A rifle cracked in the rocks directly ahead of Longarm.

Grabbing his Winchester, he flung himself from his horse. Another shot whipped past his cheek as he ran toward a clump of boulders beside the trail. As he neared the rocks, lead began whining off them like angry hornets. He dove for cover behind the nearest boulder and cranked a shell into his Winchester's firing chamber.

The trouble was, he could not find anyone to shoot at. Suddenly, a lean fellow with a pencil-thin mustache stepped forward and kicked him in the chin. Longarm felt himself go hurtling back, his Colt clattering to the stony ground . . .

Also in the LONGARM series from Jove

LONGARM
LONGARM IN SILVER CITY
LONGARM ON THE BARBARY COAST
LONGARM AND THE MOONSHINERS
LONGARM IN YUMA
LONGARM IN BOULDER CANYON
LONGARM IN DEADWOOD
LONGARM AND THE GREAT TRAIN ROBBERY
LONGARM AND THE LONE STAR LEGEND
LONGARM IN THE BADLANDS
LONGARM IN THE BIG THICKET
LONGARM AND THE EASTERN DUDES
LONGARM IN THE BIG BEND
LONGARM AND THE SNAKE DANCERS
LONGARM ON THE GREAT DIVIDE
LONGARM AND THE BUCKSKIN ROGUE
LONGARM AND THE CALICO KID
LONGARM AND THE FRENCH ACTRESS
LONGARM AND THE OUTLAW LAWMAN
LONGARM AND THE LONE STAR VENGEANCE
LONGARM AND THE BOUNTY HUNTERS
LONGARM IN NO MAN'S LAND
LONGARM AND THE BIG OUTFIT
LONGARM AND SANTA ANNA'S GOLD
LONGARM AND THE CUSTER COUNTY WAR
LONGARM IN VIRGINIA CITY
LONGARM AND THE LONE STAR BOUNTY
LONGARM AND THE JAMES COUNTY WAR
LONGARM AND THE CATTLE BARON
LONGARM AND THE STEER SWINDLERS
LONGARM AND THE HANGMAN'S NOOSE
LONGARM AND THE OMAHA TINHORNS
LONGARM AND THE DESERT DUCHESS
LONGARM ON THE PAINTED DESERT
LONGARM ON THE OGALLALA TRAIL
LONGARM ON THE ARKANSAS DIVIDE
LONGARM AND THE BLIND MAN'S VENGEANCE
LONGARM AT FORT RENO
LONGARM AND THE DURANGO PAYROLL
LONGARM WEST OF THE PECOS
LONGARM ON THE NEVADA LINE
LONGARM AND THE BLACKFOOT GUNS
LONGARM ON THE SANTA CRUZ
LONGARM AND THE LONE STAR RESCUE
LONGARM AND THE COWBOY'S REVENGE
LONGARM ON THE GOODNIGHT TRAIL
LONGARM AND THE FRONTIER DUCHESS
LONGARM IN THE BITTERROOTS
LONGARM AND THE TENDERFOOT
LONGARM AND THE STAGECOACH BANDITS
LONGARM AND THE BIG SHOOT-OUT
LONGARM AND THE LONE STAR DELIVERANCE

TABOR EVANS

A JOVE BOOK

LONGARM IN THE HARD ROCK COUNTRY

A Jove Book/published by arrangement with
the author

PRINTING HISTORY
Jove edition/February 1986

ISBN: 0-515-08461-1

Jove books are published by The Berkley Publishing Group,
200 Madison Avenue, New York, N.Y. 10016.

PRINTED IN THE UNITED STATES OF AMERICA

LONGARM

IN THE HARD ROCK COUNTRY

Chapter 1

Longarm cursed and fired at the fleeing outlaw. Then he fired again, hopelessly, furiously.

Turning, he raced back for the big chestnut, hauled himself up into his saddle, and gave the animal his head. The horse picked its way swiftly down the rocky, shale-littered slope, as the firing came again from the canyon rim above him. The horse reached the canyon floor and lengthened his stride. Longarm bent low over the animal's neck as the bullets whined past his head like angry hornets. But a moment later, Longarm had put the canyon behind him.

Tomlinson was only a fast-moving target now as he sped over the parkland ahead of him, and though for a while it appeared that Longarm's chestnut was gaining on Tomlinson's powerful bay, it soon became clear to the lawman that his mount was no match for Tomlinson's, and the outlaw began to pull away steadily.

The parkland soon gave way to islands of timber, and finally, far in the distance, to pine-clad foothills. Longarm realized that if he didn't overtake Tomlinson before he reached those foothills, he would more than likely end up striding into Vail's office with used-up travel vouchers—and no Jed Tomlinson.

Not long after, with Longarm still losing ground, the outlaw vanished into a heavy stand of timber clothing a foothill half a mile or so ahead. Longarm pulled his nearly foundering horse to a halt. On all sides of him were foothills clothed in pine and aspen. Tomlinson was up in there somewhere, moving swiftly and silently away from Longarm. But there was no telling in which direction he was going—and the pine needles carpeting those slopes would leave few, if any, tracks for him to follow.

For the moment, at least, Longarm had lost his man.

He turned his horse and headed back to the badlands, and those who had opened up on him from the canyon rim.

It was close to dusk when Longarm caught sight of two riders crossing a flat below him. They were moving away from the same patch of badlands where Longarm had lost Tomlinson. One was astride a black, the other a sorrel. A single look was all Longarm needed. These two were the men who had fired on him. In Twin Rocks, where Longarm had picked up his prisoner, the sheriff had pointed out these same two riders as Tomlinson's sidekicks. All the while Longarm had been in Twin Rocks, the two had kept their distance, waiting. They had ridden out a few hours before sunup the morning Longarm had set out for Denver with his prisoner.

Longarm dismounted and watched the two riders. They were heading southwest, taking the same direction as Tomlinson had when he bolted. It didn't take Longarm any time at all to figure it out—and then to marvel grudgingly at how well the three of them had worked it out.

A year before, a Denver court had convicted Tomlinson of robbing a stage and killing the messenger guard. He had been sentenced to hang, but during his transfer to the local jail, with the aid of accomplices, he had made his escape.

When Jed Tomlinson had been apprehended by an alert local sheriff in Twin Rocks, Billy Vail had sent Longarm to bring him back. Since there was no longer a rail link or a stage line connecting the played-out mining town to the rest of Colorado, Longarm had to ride in alone and ride out with his prisoner.

Tomlinson had been a surprisingly quiet and almost docile prisoner. So when he complained that Longarm's handcuffs were cutting into his wrists, Longarm had agreed to let the man ride with his wrists unmanacled. When, a few minutes later, they rode into the canyon, Tomlinson had lagged slightly behind Longarm—until the first shot came from above. Then, whipping his horse furiously, Tomlinson raced past Longarm, knocked the lawman from his horse, and bolted down the canyon.

Now, watching those two men below him, Longarm carefully backed off and remounted. Keeping out of sight just below the ridge line so as not to present a silhouette, he followed them as they continued on toward the dark ramparts crowding the western horizon.

The two men were deep in the foothills when they finally made camp. Longarm made his own camp a dry one and much higher than theirs, beyond a ridge. Building a fire only large enough to warm his coffee and thaw some of his sourdough biscuits, Longarm slept fitfully, woke before dawn, and hunkered down into a patch of brush just above the outlaws' camp.

Custis Long was his full name, but all those who knew him well enough called him Longarm. He was a big man, better than six feet tall, who loomed giant-like in the predawn darkness. His friends were likely to josh him about a man his size being likely to spook livestock and make people thoughtful. On the comfortable side of forty, his lean, lantern-jawed face bore the stamp of one who has endured many years of blistering sun and cutting winds since reaching Colorado as a young man from West-by-God-Virginia. The resulting raw-boned features were brown enough for those of an Indian. Indeed, if it were not for the gunmetal blue of his wide-set eyes, the tobacco-leaf color of his hair, and the waxed longhorn mustache he favored, he could easily have been mistaken for an unusually tall Indian. He stirred impatiently, stood up, then picked his way silently a few feet farther down the slope to get a closer look at the two outlaws.

The tallest one, his lean face bronzed and beardless, appeared to be the leader. He was the one riding the black, a color he obviously favored. His riding boots and his flat-crowned plains hat were black also, as were his tight-fitting pants and gun holster. He wore a buttonless black leather vest, and from the way his white shirt reflected the firelight, Longarm was sure it was silk.

His partner, the one who rode the sorrel, was a broad-beamed, chunky fellow with a beard and whiskey-raw features who moved about the campfire with a truculent heaviness, banging cups and the coffee pot incessantly. His voice seemed to carry farther, also, and he was forever mopping his beefy features or pulling down on the brim of his black hat, as if he were afraid he were going to lose it. He wore faded Levi's and a checked shirt under a tattered vest—all in all, a strangely inappropriate companion for the other one, Longarm would have thought.

The two men set out at the crack of dawn, and by noon

Longarm was watching them ride across the floor of a high valley on their way toward a mining town squatting in the lap of shadowy foothills.

Longarm waited until the two reached the town before descending from a steep slope and heading after them. It was dusk when he rode into the town, and the sky overhead was already awash with stars. He had heard of this place. Built with its shabby backside hard against a towering mountain, it was called Green's Creek. Its best days were past, and Longarm was surprised to find the place looking so prosperous.

He clopped loudly onto a plank bridge that carried him across a creek and before long found himself riding past single-story frame dwellings, their lights blooming feebly through dusty windows. Other buildings were scattered about on the slopes surrounding the town. As he moved on down the street, he could hear the town's deep, muffled heartbeat—a booming stamping mill on a hill high above the town. Halfway down the street another road cut out of the hills to form an intersection. A hotel, the Travelers' Rest, a general store, and two saloons faced each other across the intersection. Beyond the town itself the road met a canyon and vanished into the mountain's sheer slopes, the shadow of which lay hard on the town.

As Longarm rode through the intersection, he glimpsed a black and a sorrel standing at the hitch rails in front of the Miners' Palace. He did not see the big gray Tomlinson was riding. Without pause, he rode on past the saloon and dismounted in front of the livery.

An old man drifted out of the stable's rear darkness. "Third stall back."

Longarm gave the chestnut a drink at the street trough, then led him into the stall and removed his saddle. He stayed in the stall long enough to wipe off the chestnut's sweat-gummed back, then left the barn and unwrapped a cheroot, lighting up as he went. The smoke had no flavor in his parched mouth and he bent down over the drinking trough's feed pipe and let the water roll into his throat and fill his stomach until he could hold no more.

Then he straightened and kept going on down the street until he reached the Miners' Palace. The black and the sorrel were still at the hitch rack. He strode through the batwings, paused a moment to get the lay of the place, then shouldered himself up to the bar and asked for a bottle of Maryland rye. The bartender had none, so he accepted a bottle of whiskey instead, turned, and surveyed the crowded saloon.

Though the two men he was following had left their horses in front, Longarm saw no sign of them. He poured himself a drink, slapped the shot glass down onto the bar, and left. Once on the porch, he caught the sudden odor of food from the Travelers' Rest hotel on the corner, its effect so sharp that a pain started in the corners of his jaws. A steady stream of men were filing in and out of the hotel dining room. Flicking away his cheroot, Longarm crossed the street to the livery stable.

A moment later, his saddlebags and other gear slung over one shoulder, his Winchester in his left hand, Longarm left the livery stable and crossed to the hotel. He registered, climbed to the second floor, and entered his room. Dumping his gear on the bed, he took off his snuff-brown Stetson and shrugged out of his tobacco-brown frock coat. Folding the coat carefully, he placed it down on the bedspread. He was careful not to drop his watch or let the derringer slip from the watch-fob pocket when he took off his vest. Next came his cross-draw rig, heavy with his double-action Colt Model T .44-40.

Stripping off his shirt, he poured water from the pitcher into the washbasin, then busied himself scrubbing the heavy layer of grime off his face and neck, promising himself a long, steaming bath first thing in the morning. After drying himself off, he slapped the dust from his shirt and shrugged back into it.

A moment later, fully dressed and well armed, he went downstairs to the hotel dining room, found a table, and ordered his meal. Then he sat back, lit another cheroot, and looked the place over, relishing in the luxury of a solid seat under him at last and a fully cooked meal on the way.

"May I sit down?"

Longarm looked up. A Chinese woman was standing by his table. He had been looking in the other direction and had not noticed her approaching his table. His first, fleeting impression was that she was beautiful—astonishingly so.

"Here?" he asked, frowning. "At my table?"

"If you don't mind."

He was on his feet instantly, his big hands pulling out a chair. As she sat, he moved it deftly in for her, at the same time cursing himself for not having found a way somehow to have taken a bath. Despite the abbreviated toilet he had managed upstairs, he was acutely aware that he still stank of the trail.

"Thank you," she said. "You are very kind."

"It is my pleasure. I don't like to eat alone, Miss . . . ?"

"Wong."

"Miss Wong. And I am Custis Long."

"Shall I call you Custis?"

"That would be fine."

"Then you may call me Lotus."

Longarm smiled. "I have already ordered, Lotus, but I'll be glad to wait for your dinner to arrive."

"Thank you, but there's no need for that. You are indeed a gentleman, Custis, but I have already eaten. Would you mind if I just sat here and kept you company while you ate?"

"Of course not." Longarm leaned back in his chair, took out a cheroot, and lit it. "You speak pretty good English, Lotus."

She smiled and bowed her head slightly in acknowledgement of his compliment. "Before coming to this benighted land," she explained, "my home was in San Francisco, where I served as the governess to the children of a Baptist minister. You see, my father was the captain of a clipper ship engaged in the tea trade with China. It was in Canton that he met my mother and in San Francisco where he made his home on retiring."

Longarm saw her look inquiringly at his cheroot, and immediately dug into his pocket and offered her one. She bit off the tip expertly and leaned forward. As he lit her cheroot, he found himself studying her closely.

The only trace he could find of that Yankee sea captain was her incredible blue eyes. All the rest of her was Chinese, pure and unadulterated—high cheekbones, olive complexion, delicate features, and a sleek, sinuous figure, all of it enhanced by a barely perceptible scent that spoke of centuries spent in the art of seducing men.

Lotus smiled suddenly at his intent perusal, her teeth gleaming like pearls behind her ruby lips.

"You shouldn't smoke," he told her.

"I know," she said, shrugging. "But there are many things I should not do."

"Like sitting down with a stranger?"

"Yes."

"Then why did you?"

"You are in grave danger."

"That so?"

At that moment Longarm's meal arrived. Lotus sat back and watched him eat it. At last, his meal finished, the dishes cleared away, Longarm ordered coffee. At his gentle insistence to order something so she might join him at least in this, Lotus capitulated graciously and ordered tea.

"All right," Longarm said, leaning back and fixing Lotus with a cold, appraising glance, "now that the condemned man has finished his last meal, he would like to know why you said he was in grave danger."

"Of course. You followed two men into town, did you not?"

"I did."

"Those two men are well known here. One of them is a gambler at the Miners' Palace, the other is his sidekick."

"They have names?"

"Jake Sharlow is the gambler and Biff Grunewald is his companion."

"What's the name of the tall one?"

"Sharlow. He's the gambler. He is also very quick with a gun."

Longarm nodded. "And his sidekick—the short, stumpy fellow—would be Biff Grunewald."

"Yes."

"Okay. So what about them?"

"They are waiting for you to leave this dining room."

"Where are they waiting?"

"Outside somewhere. I'm not sure exactly."

"There's a redhead," Longarm told Lotus. "A wild rawboned son of a bitch. Freckled, quick to anger. His name is Jed Tomlinson. I figured Sharlow and Grunewald were going to meet him here. Have you seen him anywhere in town?"

"Look behind you, Custis."

Longarm did. Jed Tomlinson was sitting at a table in the corner, next to the door leading onto the back alley. His hat was on the table, covering his right hand.

Longarm had no doubt what Tomlinson was clutching under that hat.

Swinging back to Lotus, for the first time Longarm noticed how quickly the crowd in the dining room had thinned out. The frightened, drawn looks on the waitress's faces were also quite noticeable, and even as Longarm realized this, he saw his own waitress approaching the table with his check.

Taking it from her, he saw how her hand shook. He paid the waitress, then put his hat on and stood up.

"What about you?" he asked Lotus. "They will know you've just warned me."

"This is my hotel." She smiled. "When I heard what they were up to, I told them I would warn you—that I wanted no gunplay in my hotel. You will please go outside now, Custis."

Longarm nodded, a wry smile on his lean face. She was a cool one. She had made a deal with Jed Tomlinson and his sidekicks. She would send Longarm out of her hotel to keep them from breaking in, guns blazing. A very practical and level-headed young lady.

Longarm touched the brim of his hat to Lotus and strode from the dining room. A moment before he reached the front door, he glanced back through the arch. Tomlinson was no longer at his table, and the back door was swinging shut. Turning back around, Longarm strode quickly toward the hotel's front door.

Outside it was, then.

Chapter 2

Stepping out onto the hotel porch, Longarm found the street was now completely deserted. The windows of a store across the street stared unblinkingly back at him like the empty sockets in a bleached skull. Unholstering his Colt, he stepped off the porch and headed up the street toward the stable. If worse came to worst, he might be able to find cover in there.

The tall one—the gambler, Sharlow—stepped out of the alley alongside the hotel. As Longarm dropped to one knee, Sharlow fired. Crabbing sideways, Longarm returned his fire until the jutting porch obscured his vision.

Heavy running footsteps came at Longarm from behind. Whirling, Longarm fired up at the short one, Grunewald, punching a neat hole in his shirt. Yet still Grunewald came on, his feet moving mechanically. Ducking aside, Longarm let the man crash into the porch just as a fusillade opened up on him from across the street. The gunman—Tomlinson, more than likely—was crouched behind two barrels. As the rounds pounded into the porch supports and steps, Longarm threw himself flat and squeezed off two quick shots. As his return fire slammed into the barrels, Tomlinson darted out from behind them and ducked down a nearby alley.

But where was Sharlow? Still flat on the ground, Longarm pushed himself back until he was under the porch. In the dim light from the street lamps, Longarm could see the figure of Grunewald sprawled about ten feet in front of the porch, his eyes staring blindly in under the porch at him.

Longarm heard the sound of boots crunching on sand to his left. Turning his head, he caught sight of a pair of boots moving stealthily out from behind the hotel. It was Sharlow. The gambler was peering across the empty hotel porch at the street, looking for signs of Longarm. Longarm moved his gun hand slowly to the left, aimed at Sharlow's closest boot, and fired. He saw the slug kick into the expensive black leather just above the ankle bone.

There was a muffled cry as Sharlow came down hard. Longarm saw him hit the ground, then try to scramble to his feet. As Longarm darted out from under the porch to finish off Sharlow, a second fusillade came at Longarm from the mouth of an alley beside the livery stable. Ducking back quickly, Longarm saw Tomlinson, astride one horse and leading another, charge boldly out of the alley and head directly for the hotel. Flinging up his Colt, Longarm tracked him, and fired.

His hammer came down on an empty chamber.

Longarm cursed. The range was too great for his derringer. Swiftly, he swung out his Colt's gate and reloaded. By the time he had finished, however, the crippled Sharlow had managed to fling himself up onto the second horse and was galloping out of town with Tomlinson. Even though he was forced to ride with one foot held awkwardly out of the stirrup, he somehow managed to stay on the galloping horse. Longarm raced out into the center of the street and sent one last hopeless round after the two. Then he pulled up wearily and watched them disappear.

A hefty-looking fellow in his fifties approached. Hatless, he was wearing a well-tailored black frock coat with a string tie knotted at his throat. He sported a set of reddish mutton-chop whiskers. His gray eyes were narrow and shifty, but his smile was a broad one. Behind him the townsmen were gathering quickly.

Sticking out his hand, the man cried, "Pleased to meet you, mister! That was some fine gunplay, fighting off three men like that. My name's Malcolm Hartridge."

"Custis Long," Longarm replied, shaking the man's hand.

"I am head of the town council," Hartridge told Longarm. "You mind telling me what this here ruckus was all about?"

"I'm a deputy U. S. marshal, Hartridge," Longarm replied. "One of those men is wanted for killing a shotgun guard."

"That so? Well, now, which one would that be?"

"The redhead. Jed Tomlinson."

Hartridge seemed perfectly satisfied with this explanation. He glanced quickly about him at the townsmen crowding close, listening to every word. As he prepared to address them, they waited expectantly.

"You hear that, men?" he cried. "That scalawag Jed Tomlinson was a killer! Wanted for murder!"

Hartridge turned back to Longarm. "Well, sir, I was about to ask if you might consider becoming our town marshal, but I see you already have employment. As soon as you've had time to catch your breath, I would be honored to join you in the Miners' Palace, the drinks on me, of course."

"If I have the time, Hartridge," Longarm told him.

He left the man and pushed his way through the crowd toward the hotel. Only when he reached its porch did he realize he had been hit. The bullet had creased the back of his upper arm, cutting through his frock coat and shirt. Though the wound was not bleeding, it burned a little. Judging from the angle the bullet must have taken, Longarm could not imagine how it had missed slamming into his side.

"Were you wounded?" Lotus asked urgently as she stepped quickly to the edge of the porch, one lank handyman and a few other hotel employees crowding about her.

"Nothing to worry about," Longarm told her. He mounted the porch and pushed past the hotel's employees into the lobby. Behind him in the street outside, the crowd continued to build. Longarm could hear excited accounts of the gun battle being shouted back and forth across the street.

Lotus had remained at his side, still obviously concerned about his flesh wound. He looked down at her. "You mind telling me where a man can get a bath in this town after dark?"

She smiled up at him. "Go to your room. I will see to it."

"Thanks."

Longarm moved past her and mounted the stairs to his room.

A thin, birdlike woman, her sleeves pushed up, began lugging steaming buckets of water into Longarm's room. Again and again the charwoman entered with new steaming buckets. Longarm was astonished at their number. Finally a high-backed tub was brought in, the outside of which was decorated with lilies and other flowers, with a few birds here and there perched on branches. It was a tub which obviously belonged to a woman. Stepping close to it as the charwoman began dumping the scalding water into the tub, he realized he would be cramped some when he slid down into it, his knees reaching clear to his nose. But he didn't care. A bath was what he needed and he was grateful for it.

The charwoman left him with a sponge, a bar of soap, and a brush for scrubbing his back. He yanked off his boots, peeled out of his clothes, and approached the tub gingerly. Steam was curling up off the water's surface. Gritting his teeth, he stepped in, almost cried out, then slowly eased himself into the near-scalding water. In a moment, sweat was pouring off his forehead and he was happily soaping himself down with the sponge. So intent was he that he did not hear Lotus enter the room. The first he knew of her presence was the sudden, unexpected cascade of steaming water she poured down over his head and shoulders.

Gasping for breath, Longarm clawed at the sides of the tub and pushed himself erect. Lotus was standing beside him in a long red robe. There was an impish smile on her face.

"Don't get out," she told him softly as she picked up the sponge and soaped it. "Stand there and let me get your back—and the rest of you."

As she scrubbed away at the backs of his legs and thighs, she did not seem to notice or care that he was standing before her stark naked. Humming merrily, she worked away at the small of his back, his buttocks, and then turned her attention to the front of him, her hands enclosed in a soapy cloth as she vigorously cleaned his crotch.

By the time she had finished with him, it was obvious that Longarm had become aware of her as a woman.

"How is your wound?" she inquired.

"Tender."

"The rest of you looks fine."

"I'm glad you approve."

A slight smile on her face, she pushed him gently back down into the tub, soaped his head thoroughly until his hair was heavy with suds, then dumped another bucket of hot water over him. It took still another bucket to wash away all the suds, and as he was sputtering to get his breath once again, she leaned her face close to his and finished off the area around his crotch.

"Stand up," she commanded softly.

He stood. She dumped the last bucket over him, then patted his shoulders and head dry. Then she moved back while he stepped out of the tub. Then she finished drying him off. The job finally completed, she draped the towel over the back of the tub and surveyed his clean, bright nakedness.

He was reaching for something to cover himself—especially his straining erection—when she untied her sash and opened her robe. There was nothing under it but her sleek, olive body, her pubic patch as black as coal. It appeared to be already moist and a faint, indefinable scent was emanating from her. He felt his erection lifting eagerly.

"I thought I might like you a little better if you were clean," she said. "All of you. Now I am ready."

The smoky blue of her eyes grew smokier as she opened her arms to him. He went for her, swept her up in his arms, and deposited her on the bedspread.

"The window shades are up," she whispered. "Turn off the lamps."

He left her to turn them off, and when he returned her legs were wide, her arms open for him.

"Mmm," she murmured. "I can see you are ready. Bathing you got me ready, too. I warn you, Custis, don't hold back. Hurry!"

Longarm didn't hold back.

It was an hour later. The stamping mill was still thudding on the hill above the town, its steady thump imparting an ominous beat to the night and all who moved through it.

Though Lotus had taken all Longarm had, she was not anxious to leave his bed. At the moment he was savoring that delicious empty feeling that fell over him whenever he had been thoroughly satisfied. Still in his arms, Lotus was murmuring softly into his ears, her fingers tracing magical patterns over his chest. Every now and then they would investigate the area past his belly button.

"So Green's Creek doesn't have a marshal," Longarm said after a while.

"The town fathers tried that a couple of years ago. They picked a young miner eager to wear a tin star. The poor kid didn't last a week."

"Who runs things?"

"That man you spoke to in the street. Malcolm Hartridge. He runs the town and the stamping mill and the four silver mines still producing in the area."

"Silver?"

"Yes. Most of the gold has played out, but the silver mines are still holding up."

"You say Hartridge runs them. Who owns them?"

"I have heard his name once or twice. Dr. Fell, some call him. His full name is Dr. Han Chow Fell."

"Then he's Chinese."

"Yes."

"Does he live in the town here?"

"No. He lives in the mountains . . . somewhere."

Longarm saw that Lotus was becoming uneasy, as if she had already revealed to Longarm more than was wise. "You sure as hell make him sound mysterious," he observed.

"But he *is* mysterious. And dangerous. I do not like to discuss him, Longarm." As she spoke, she shuddered slightly.

Longarm was more than a little curious about this Dr. Fell and anxious to find out more about him, but he realized it would do no good to press Lotus on it. "All right, then," he said. "Enough about this mysterious Dr. Fell. But maybe you *can* tell me where Tomlinson and Sharlow might have headed."

She plucked idly at his earlobes. "Perhaps I can. There is talk around that Tomlinson and Sharlow have been working a small gold claim in the mountains."

"Where?"

"Northwest of here."

"You can't be any more specific than that?"

"I do not know if I should be."

"Why?"

She frowned, as if pondering whether or not to tell him. While she was thinking it over, she rested her hand on his belly, the warmth of it spreading magically all the way to his groin.

He stirred uneasily. "Come on. Tell me."

She sighed. "I don't know if I can trust you, Custis."

"You mind telling me why?"

"You say you are a U. S. marshal. Yet you did such a foolish thing when first you rode into Green's Creek."

"Foolish?"

"Yes," she retorted, "foolish. Very foolish. Everyone talks of it. You must have known those men were here in Green's Creek, yet you rode openly into town and made no effort to stay out of sight. Then you walked into the Miners' Palace, even though you must have seen Sharlow's and Grunewald's horses standing out front."

"Yes, I saw them."

"Still, you walked into the saloon as bold as brass. Did you think those men were going to lay down their guns at sight of you?"

"Nope."

"Then why did you do it?"

Longarm chuckled. "I was advertising."

"Advertising?" She frowned at him and propped her cheek

on her hand. "What on earth do you mean?"

"If Tomlinson was here waiting for them, I didn't want them running off. I wanted them to know I was here—and that I was alone. That I could be taken. Otherwise, they might just disappear into those mountains and I'd never find them again."

She shook her head in wonder. "So you deliberately made yourself a target."

"Something like that. Yes."

"And then you went to dinner at my hotel."

"Yes. I was famished."

"Did you know by that time that almost everyone in town knew there was going to be trouble?"

Longarm shrugged. "Is that when you spoke to them?"

"Yes. I spoke to Tomlinson. I told him I did not want my hotel to become a shooting gallery. I promised him that I could make sure you went out the front door when you finished eating."

"How could you promise that? I might have decided to go upstairs after my meal."

She smiled. "Not after I told you they were out there waiting for you."

"But what made you so sure I'd go out the *front* door?"

She dropped her lips to his chest. "That was easy. By letting Tomlinson in the back door, and giving him that table in front of it."

He squinted down at her. "You are a crafty one."

"I am pleased," she responded. "You did not call me inscrutable."

He lifted her head off his chest and kissed her on the lips. They answered hungrily, then began moving passionately over his face, his neck, and all the while her incredible fingers were sending flame through his loins. To his astonishment, he felt himself quicken eagerly, his erection lifting once again.

As she slid one silken limb over his left thigh, she felt it too and he heard her happy chuckle. In an instant she was astride him, sinking deliciously down onto his shaft with wondrous ease. As she straightened up and accepted him so deep, she gasped.

Her eyes alight, Lotus began to ride him like a pony, a trotting pony, her head thrown back, her marvelously firm, upthrust breasts rocking too, her hair an inky cloud coiling about her head. Before long, he was impelled to play a more active role. Tightening his buttocks, he found himself driving up to meet her thrust for thrust as she ground herself down upon him, mewing softly now with each movement.

He ran his hands up and down her spine, feeling the bones riding under her silken skin. His own urgency heightened rapidly and he started pulling her down upon him as he rose to meet each of her downstrokes. Soon he was handling her roughly, using her with rough abandon in an effort to set off the fire building in his groin. Still, no matter how violently they rocked and clawed at each other, her inner muscles held his erection like a searing vise.

At last she shuddered, grew rigid, and flung her head back, letting out a sharp cry, like a large cat. Her orgasm continued for an incredibly long while, as she tapped into a reservoir of lust deep within her. Groaning, caught up in her wild pulsing, her lips found his, her tongue thrusting like something alive deep into his mouth. The smell of her was intoxicating, as was the sound of her eager panting. She was all silk and claws now, lust unhitched from all traces, wild, unrestrained.

Aroused now beyond anything he had experienced in a long time, Longarm took charge. He rolled Lotus over and plunged still more deeply into her. Astonished and delighted at his own resurgent abandon, she gasped with delight and at once her legs rose to lock firmly around his buttocks. Part of her now, grafted to her flesh, he moved swiftly further up onto the bed for a better purchase. Pleased at the sight of her tossing head, her wide eyes, the deep guttural grunts that exploded from her with each long, powerful thrust.

Abruptly, she climaxed, moaning, her nails raking down his back. Longarm let himself go completely now, pounding into her with a sudden, wild ferocity as he neared his own climax.

She growled at him angrily. "You bastard! You're outlasting me! Wait for me! Wait for me!"

Longarm chuckled and closed his eyes. For him, the game was already finished as he plunged on over the top. He experienced a long, shuddering orgasm, and for a delicious moment it felt as if all of him were being sucked deep inside her.

He savored the sweet lassitude for a moment or two longer, one big hand under her buttocks holding her close. Then he eased gently off her. She lay on her back, panting, tiny beads of perspiration covering her entire body. A lock of black hair was plastered to her brow. She turned her head and he saw her large almond-shaped eyes regarding him.

He closed his eyes and dropped into a deep, dreamless nap. When he awoke, she had propped her head up on her hand and was studying him intently. Still feeling good, he winked at her.

"Tomorrow," she said after a while, "will you go after Jed Tomlinson?"

"That's the idea. With Sharlow wounded, they won't get very far."

She thought a long moment, her gaze distant. Longarm waited, aware she was coming to a difficult decision. At last she turned to him. "I think maybe I know where Sharlow and Tomlinson might be."

"I'd sure appreciate you telling me, Lotus."

"There's a canyon. At the end of it is Sharlow's cabin.

You'll have to go through a little town called Maria. It's not much now. The mine nearby's all played out."

"I appreciate you telling me this, Lotus."

"I'm just being selfish," she responded, smiling lustily at him. "I want you to come back to Green's Creek alive. Maybe next time I'll outlast you."

"Don't count on it."

She laughed and snuggled closer. He put his arms around her, flipped the covers over them both, and sank into sleep.

As the sun broke over the mountains the next morning, Longarm was already high above Green's Creek, urging his chestnut on into the timber. He was heading for Maria, the old mining camp Lotus had mentioned. She had warned him to be careful when he entered it, reminding him that by then he would be in country that harbored many other men of Sharlow and Tomlinson's persuasion. When he had asked about the canyon where Sharlow had his mine, she had told him it was at least ten miles beyond Maria, with Sharlow's cabin on a slope at the far end of the steep, sheer-walled canyon.

A little before noon, he broke out above the timberline and made his noon camp beside a cold, shallow stream, the thin air catching in his lungs. He dined on sourdough biscuits washed down with coffee, then moved out, following a narrow trail that dropped finally into a mile-wide, bowl-like depression in the mountains. By mid-afternoon he passed below the timberline once more, found himself following a weed-filled, deeply rutted road, and kept on it until he came in sight of Maria.

He drifted forward with caution, observing that the town of Maria was little more than a huddle of old shacks split by the road he had been following. Against the nearby hillside, he made out the yellow scars of mine dumps and the scaffolding of buildings stripped of their covering timber.

When he reached the side of an outlying building, he stopped in its shadow to peer carefully at the town. Ahead of him he saw a two-storied building with an outside stairway leading from the street to the second floor. There appeared to be a saloon on the ground floor with a few horses standing before it. Across the road from the saloon stood another large building whose windows and doors had been boarded up.

He studied the horses. They were uncommonly fine mounts, and one of them—a black—looked as if it had been ridden hard, judging from the high gloss of perspiration on its quivering flanks. He saw a gray as well. He remained in his saddle for a few minutes, watching carefully. A vaguely familiar figure left the saloon as Jed Tomlinson crossed from the boarded-up building and went into the saloon past him.

Longarm gave Tomlinson a good ten minutes or so. Then he nudged the horse to a slow walk, left the building's shadow, and moved back out into the road. Dismounting finally before the saloon, he dropped his reins over the hitch rail and went inside. Four men sat at a table playing poker. All four ceased playing and looked at him with a dead steadiness out of eyes shaded with low hatbrims. One of the four rose and moved behind the small bar. He lifted a bottle and a shot glass down and set it before Longarm on the counter.

"Where can a man eat around here?" Longarm asked.

The saloonkeeper indicated a back room with his thumb. "Go in there. I'll fix it."

"Where would a man sleep?"

"Take your bedroll up the outside stairs and pick a bunk."

"I'll eat first," Longarm said, and poured himself a drink. The saloonkeeper vanished into the back room.

The three other men hadn't stirred since his entrance. One of them had a pencil-thin mustache, and all three had swarthy complexions, unkempt hair and lean, hungry faces—

like wolves who had been searching fruitlessly for fresh game through a long winter.

Longarm took up the bottle and glass and walked into the back room, where he saw a table covered with a red oilcloth. There was a plate on the table with a steak half cut through and a cup of coffee overturned, the dregs of the coffee still spreading over the oilcloth. A chair stood away from the table, where it had been hurriedly kicked aside, and the door leading outside hung open.

Longarm slapped the bottle and glass down on the table and in three quick strides darted through the open doorway. Glancing to his right, he saw Tomlinson's back hurrying around behind the boarded-up building across the street.

Behind him, the saloonkeeper stepped out through the door and barked, "You want that meal now?"

"I'll tell you when I get back," Longarm said, unholstering his Colt.

He darted across the street and kept going until he reached the weed-grown back alley behind the boarded-up building. He saw no one. Two privies squatted low in the gathering dusk. Longarm glanced up at the building and saw that the boards covering one window had been ripped off. Anyone behind it commanded the road and the rest of the town. From that position a man could see clearly anyone entering or leaving the town. But he could not see straight down, not at the spot where Longarm now held himself against the wall.

Spotting a doorway, he moved swiftly to it, pushed open the door, and stepped inside. He found himself in a narrow hallway with stairs a little to the right leading to the second floor. He moved to the stairs and paused, waiting. The dry, musty smell of the abandoned place fell over him. Keeping perfectly still, he was aware of no sound besides that of his own breathing—until he heard the scurrying, gritty sound of a rat fleeing across an upstairs room. A second later the silence returned, more complete than before.

Longarm set one foot down carefully on the first step, testing it. He let his weight fall easy and slow, and tested the next step with his other foot. It made only the slightest sound, but it was enough to make him pause. After a moment he continued on up the stairs, resting the soles of his boots only on the edge of each stair.

Reaching the second floor, he paused. The darkness was so profound that he was only barely able to make out partitions and doors. He waited for his eyes to get accustomed to the darkness and was aware of no one else in the room as he stood there—except for a sudden coolness brushing the back of his neck.

At once he started across the room toward an open door on the opposite side. Before he reached it, a voice came at him from out of the black doorway.

"That you, Long?"

Longarm held up, recognizing Jed Tomlinson's voice instantly. "Yeah, Tomlinson. It's me. Throw your gun out."

"Hell, why should I? The trap's been set and you just took the bait!"

Longarm heard someone behind him. Whoever it was must have been in a room at the top of the stairs—and when he opened the door, it had caused the coolness on the back of Longarm's neck.

So Longarm could not go back.

Firing straight ahead of him, he lowered his shoulder and plunged toward the doorway. Tomlinson's gun thundered back at him. Longarm felt the slug burn past. A startled cry of pain erupted behind him, but Longarm paid no attention as his lowered shoulder slammed into someone standing in the doorway and knocked him violently aside.

Longarm heard a startled grunt, followed by a bitter curse as the man he hit slammed hard to the floor. A shadowy figure lunged at him from his left. Swinging his Colt around,

Longarm clubbed the man fiercely, slamming him back against the wall. Following up on his blow, Longarm beat the man back as the fellow tried to club Longarm senseless. Longarm shook off the blows easily and slammed the man's head back against the wall with his forearm, then fired into his chest and stepped back.

As the fellow crumpled at Longarm's feet, the one he had knocked to the floor an instant before fled out the door. A second later Longarm heard the sound of booted feet piling down the stairs.

Ripping aside a couple of boards, Longarm thrust his head out through the window in time to see Tomlinson dart out into the alley. Longarm got off only one shot before Tomlinson vanished. A moment later, Longarm heard the quick thunder of Tomlinson's horse. Pulling his head back in, Longarm bent close to the man he had shot, and found himself gazing down into Sharlow's lean face.

The gambler's eyes opened. He looked up at Longarm and said something, but Longarm could not hear him. He leaned closer.

". . . Dr. Fell! You fool!"

"What about Dr. Fell? What are you talking about, Sharlow?"

Sharlow tried to speak again, but his voice faded, his chest heaved slightly as he fought for breath. Then he died.

Longarm got to his feet. His bullet had smashed into the gambler's gut and his earlier shot in Green's Creek had turned the man's leg into an ugly swollen mess. The shin bone was shattered just above the ankle. To examine it, Sharlow must have had to cut the boot off; if he had lived, he would have lost the foot for sure. What amazed Longarm was how good a fight Sharlow had put up, despite his fearsome leg injury.

Longarm left the dead gambler and went back into the other room. His eyes acutely attuned to the darkness by this time, he had no difficulty picking out the sprawled body of the man he had heard coming at him from behind. He bent beside him and leaned his ear close to the man's heart.

The man was as dead as a fence post.

There was a black smear on his shirt just over the heart. Longarm remembered the fellow's surprised cry as the slug meant for Longarm had struck him instead. He studied the dead man's face intently. He had seen this man fleetingly in Green's Creek—where, he could not be sure—and this was the man Longarm had watched leaving the saloon earlier.

To set up the trap Tomlinson had just sprung.

Chapter 3

The three men at the poker table were gone when Longarm returned to the saloon, and the saloonkeeper was alone.

"You still want that meal?" he asked Longarm.

"Fry it up," said Longarm, pulling the chair back to the table. The saloonkeeper had righted the cup and swabbed off the oilcloth.

Fresh coffee in a clean mug, a fried steak, and fried potatoes appeared in due course, a generous four slices of thick, homemade bread added a moment later as the saloonkeeper moved past him into the saloon.

Longarm ate heartily. After a while, washing down the meal with the coffee, he asked for another cup. The saloonkeeper produced a coffee pot, still steaming, and set it down on the table.

"Join me," Longarm suggested.

The saloonkeeper eyed him a moment, then with a barely noticeable shrug dragged a chair over and sat down across from him. Pouring himself a cup, the saloonkeeper leaned back in his chair, his forefinger curled about the cup's handle, and surveyed Longarm casually. He was a man past forty with a shiny bald head, a long chin, and powerful brows. He was rangy about the shoulders, and he looked as if he might have spent his best years in the saddle.

"There's two dead men over there in that boarded-up building," Longarm said.

"I heard the shooting."

"One of them is Jake Sharlow. I don't know who the other one is, but I think maybe I seen him before in Green's Creek."

"What's he look like?"

Longarm described him as well as he could, then mentioned he had seen him leaving the saloon before he rode up.

The saloonkeeper nodded. "You stay at the Travelers' Rest, that big hotel the Dragon Lady owns?"

Longarm nodded.

"Well, that fellow you just described works for her. His name was Abe Goshen. You probably saw him around her place."

Longarm sipped his coffee and looked away from the saloonkeeper. He remembered a lank handyman standing beside Lotus when she hurried out of the hotel after the shootout. Now that Longarm recalled, this fellow also resembled the charwoman who had brought the water for his bath.

"His mother work there, too?"

The saloonkeeper shook his head. "Nope. That was Abe's sister. Funny thing, ain't it? They're almost dead ringers."

"Sharlow said something about Dr. Fell. Who the hell might that be?"

"Beats the shit out of me, mister."

"You've never heard that name before?"

"Didn't say that. Some claim he has gold mines all over the place, run by coolies. But I ain't never seen nothing to confirm that."

"You mean there are Chinese in these mountains?"

"That's how the story goes. Left over from the boom days when they was hauled in to work the gold mines for less'n a white man would. But they didn't last long. A few got strung up, and the rest was sent packin' by the miners. There's some left, maybe, but I ain't seen any. That Dragon Lady runs the hotel in Green's Creek is the only one left, as I recall."

"And Goshen worked for her."

"Yup."

"What'd he do for her?"

"Ran her errands about town. Kept the hotel fixed up." He smiled wickedly then. "Maybe once in a while she'd send him on other errands."

"Dangerous man, was he?"

"No more'n any other cornered rat."

"Did Sharlow have a cabin about ten miles from here? At the end of a canyon?"

"Nope."

"You mean it's Tomlinson's."

"I mean there ain't no cabin there now. Not any more. I know the canyon, and I know the cabin yer talkin' about. It was burnt down a year ago. If you look hard, you might find a few charred beams and some empty bean cans."

Longarm finished his coffee and dropped enough coins beside his plate to cover the meal. "What're you going to do about those two bodies in that building over there? They'll be ripe before long."

"There ain't no undertaker in this thrivin' metropolis," the saloonkeeper responded, picking at his teeth with a wood sliver, "and I don't take easy to workin' a shovel." Then he glanced behind him. "I got me some kerosene in that corner over there. I'll douse the building tomorrow mornin' and drop a match nearby. The buildin's a damn eyesore, anyway."

Longarm nodded and got to his feet. "Guess I'll see to my horse and get my bedroll."

The saloonkeeper tipped his head back to keep Longarm in view. "You're a lawman, ain't you."

Longarm saw no reason to deny it. He nodded.

"Them three gunslicks as was in here figured that pretty quick." He smiled faintly. "You have a kind of spooky way of walkin' and lookin' through a feller."

"So?"

"The thing is, them three seemed to think you might be lookin' for them."

"I'm not."

The saloonkeeper shrugged. "They don't know that for sure."

Longarm thought that over. He knew what the saloonkeeper was driving at, sure enough. The three gunslicks had heard Longarm ask the saloonkeeper about a place to sleep that night and had heard the man's reply. If he went up there now, he'd be a sleeping duck.

The saloonkeeper shrugged. "Just thought I'd mention it."

"Glad you did."

The saloonkeeper finished his coffee. Longarm tossed the man a cheroot and stepped out into the night. He would be better off sleeping on some craggy cleft for another night, it seemed, with his Colt clasped in his right hand and the cold stars winking overhead.

By mid-afternoon of the next day he was well into the canyon Lotus Wong had told him about. He found that the saloonkeeper had not exaggerated. There were only a few traces of the cabin left. It had been perched on a hillock in under a massive rock ledge. Astride the chestnut, Longarm looked around the site. Sharlow had chosen his spot well. The cabin commanded the canyon for at least two miles, and it would have taken an army to storm it.

But it was gone now.

He rode off the hillock, following a dim trail that lost itself in among the crags north of the canyon. Earlier there had been some sign indicating Tomlinson had taken this direction, and Longarm was hoping to pick up the outlaw's trail. He found nothing, however, and he was about ready to pull about and return the way he had come when a rifle cracked in the rocks directly ahead of him.

Grabbing his Winchester, Longarm flung himself from his horse. Another shot whipped past his cheek as he ran toward a clump of boulders beside the trail. As he neared the rocks, lead began whining off them like angry hornets. He dove for cover behind the nearest boulder and cranked a shell into his Winchester's firing chamber.

The trouble was, he could not find anyone to shoot at. The firing was coming at him from at least three directions. He heard the sudden rush of gravel under foot behind him and turned as a Colt thundered. He felt the Winchester kick out of his hand. As he reached across his belt for his own sixgun, a lean fellow with a pencil-thin mustache stepped forward and kicked him in the chin. Longarm felt himself go hurtling back, his Colt clattering to the stony ground.

Flat on his back, he looked up as the three men he'd seen earlier in the saloon materialized before him. He was furious—and sick and tired of being bushwhacked. The anger cleared his head. Pushing himself to a sitting position, he felt his jaw. Blood was trickling out of one corner of his mouth, and he wondered if there weren't a few teeth loose as well.

The hardcase with the thin mustache reached down and picked up Longarm's sixgun. Then he aimed it down at Longarm. His lean, wolfish companions beside him smiled. They were men who liked this sort of thing, fed on it—the way vultures feed on carrion.

"Well, Mr. Lawman," said the leader of the three, "looks like the saloonkeeper was right. You *was* headin' this way."

Longarm said nothing. Instead, he groaned and made a show of pushing himself erect to see how badly he had been injured. As he did so, he palmed the derringer from his vest pocket.

With an angry snarl, one of the men stepped forward and kicked Longarm's legs out from under him, sending Longarm sprawling down onto his face. The three men laughed loudly at Longarm's discomfiture, and one of them aimed his Colt at Longarm's foot and pulled the trigger. A geyser of sand and pebbles shot up inches from Longarm's right boot.

Ignoring this, Longarm sat up, his back braced against a boulder. Seeing this, the other outlaw jacked a fresh cartridge into his Winchester's firing chamber. Aiming quickly at Longarm's head, he squeezed the trigger, missing deliberately. But it was close enough for Longarm to feel the bullet's passage as it burned past his temple and ricocheted off the boulder.

The hardcase in charge moved in closer and went down on one knee, peering curiously at Longarm, his yellow teeth visible as he smiled suddenly and tipped his head. "You see, lawman? We got you between a rock and a hard place."

"You're making a mistake" Longarm told them, "all three of you." He kept himself bent slightly to conceal the derringer still clasped in his right palm. "I ain't after you. I got no dodgers on you three. You're making a big mistake comin' after me like this."

"Why, we're just doin' a friend of ours a favor."

"Tomlinson?"

The gunman grinned wolfishly. "Ask me no question, I tell you no lie, lawman."

"Then get it over with, you son of a bitch!" said Longarm, lashing out suddenly with his boot.

He caught the gunman on the side of his head, sending him careening backward. Longarm lifted his derringer and fired up at the hardcase with the rifle—and caught him between the eyes. Shifting the derringer an infinitesimal notch to the left, Longarm caught the other one in the neck. As the man sank to his knees, grabbing at the fountain that gouted from the wound, Longarm flung himself upon the mustachioed leader and took back his own .44.

The outlaw unsheathed his hunting knife and thrust upward. Longarm tried to pull back, but he was not fast enough, and the blade entered Longarm's side just under his left rib cage. Longarm fired down at the outlaw, grazing his left forearm. The man grimaced in pain and with maniacal persistence thrust upward again with the blade.

Longarm felt it probe deeper and strike hard against his lowest rib. As it did so, he twisted violently away. The knife went flying from the outlaw's grasp. Longarm fired his .44 a second time, this time catching the outlaw in the heart. The man sat back on his haunches suddenly, his back to a rock slab, and stared with astonishment at Longarm. Then he closed his eyes and died.

Pulling himself groggily to his feet, Longarm looked down at the blood seeping through his shirt and down his legs, then at the man he had just killed. He had the feeling he might not have killed him in time—that this time he had bought it.

He picked up his derringer and, concentrating mightily, managed to clip it back onto his gold chain. He dropped it into his right vest pocket, them attempted to drop his Colt back into his cross-draw rig. But the moment he reached across his body to do so, he felt a pain so sharp it sent windmills of light exploding before his eyes. The next thing he knew he was on his knees, the Colt still in his right hand, staring dazedly ahead of him.

By this time the first numbing shock of the knife wound had worn off, and he now became acutely aware of the searing pain enveloping his left side and swarming clear up into his lungs. So disabling was the pain, he found it difficult to breathe. He stuck his Colt in his belt and somehow managed to find his Winchester and stagger over to his horse. As he dropped the rifle into the scabbard and pulled himself up onto the horse, he realized dimly that he ought to do something to staunch the flow of blood.

He thought about it for a minute, wondering what he should do, the canyon walls spinning about his head. Impatient, his mount bobbed his head and moved ahead a few steps. Longarm tipped and slid slowly from the horse, leaving a red smear across the saddle and the horse's side. A moment later—he couldn't tell how long exactly—he found himself sitting up on the ground, watching the horse move off down the canyon toward a patch of grass.

Then he toppled over onto his side. The last thing he remembered was the sound of the horse in the distance, steadily cropping the grass.

When Running Moon first heard the shots, she had been some distance from the canyon rim, the antelope she had just shot slung over her paint's neck. Halting the pony, she lifted the old flintlock from its sling and paused, listening. The flurry of gunshots seemed to have died completely. She had known at once what that deadly rattle had meant. Men were firing at each other. The sudden silence that followed it was as ominous as the gunfire itself.

Running Moon's raven-black hair was kept off her forehead with a red headband while the rest of it flowed unencumbered to her waist. She was wearing a buckskin blouse and skirt and fine-tooled Mexican riding boots. Still listening alertly, she left the paint and started toward the rim, heading in the direction from which the gunfire had come. As she approached the rimrocks and peered down, she heard the sound of raucous, unpleasant laughter. The sound of it made her flesh creep. It was the sound some men made when they were tormenting another. She had heard such laughter often enough whenever she and her brother Black Feather visited Green's Creek.

Moving from behind a boulder to get a better view of the canyon floor, she caught sight of three men facing a fourth one lying on the ground before them. Even as she looked, she saw two of the men fire down at this one. But they missed, and their laughter told her they had missed deliberately. Her anger kindled. She was a good enough shot, but at this height and distance, she was afraid she would hit the tall one on the ground. And her flintlock fired only one shot at a time. These three men had repeating rifles and revolvers. She would be no match for them.

She told herself she would be wise to pull back and return to her horse. Black Feather had warned her more than once about the dangers of getting mixed up in white men's quarrels. Yet she could not help admiring the way the tall one defied the others. Though he was obviously close to death, he did not grovel or plead for his life.

Perhaps if she got closer, she might be able to send one shot at the three, enough to give the tall one a chance. He looked capable of taking any advantage she could provide. She looked about for a way down the steep slope so she could get closer.

A cry came from below. She glanced down in time to see the tall one kicking one of the three in the side of his head. As if by magic, a gun appeared in the tall one's hand and, with two quick shots, he cut down the other two outlaws standing over him. Transfixed, Running Moon watched as the tall one and the remaining outlaw grappled for a gun. She caught the gleam of a knife in the outlaw's hand and sucked in her breath as the blade vanished into the tall one's side. The tall one pulled back, the knife flying from his wound, and fired down at the outlaw for the second time. The outlaw flung himself back, then went very still.

Somehow, the tall one pulled himself erect, and Running Moon watched as he staggered back into the canyon for his horse. Even from where Running Moon stood, she could see the blood darkening his left thigh. More than once he stumbled, but he maintained his balance somehow and kept going.

He managed to grab his horse's reins and pull himself into his saddle. Running Moon watched intently now, for she knew a man wounded this badly could not long remain on a horse. Almost immediately the tall one slipped from his mount and collapsed to the ground. For a moment he sat up dazedly as the horse trotted a few feet down the canyon. Then he toppled over onto his side.

By this time she realized she could not allow herself to abandon such a brave man. His heart was like that of the mountain lion, and even from this distance she could see he was well-formed, his powerful body testifying to a great strength. At first Black Feather would be angry with her, but soon he would see what a fine warrior this white man was.

It took her almost half an hour to find a trail and then lead her horse down the treacherous slope. She glanced only once at the three dead men as she passed them on her way to the tall one. He was still on the ground, unconscious. After examing his wound, she wrapped a lariat around his side like a corset until the bleeding stopped. She stood back for a moment and took a deep breath before attempting to lift him up onto his saddle.

But the big man was simply too heavy for her. She thought a moment, then untied the last four strands of rope she had wrapped around his waist, looped it under Custis's shoulders, passed it over his saddle, then snubbed the end around her paint's saddlehorn. Speaking softly to her horse, she pulled it gently back and drew Custis up over his horse's saddle. Once he was draped face down over the saddle, she passed the rope under his horse and tied him on as securely as she could.

This accomplished, she went back for his hat and began the long trek to her brother's cabin.

Longarm looked up at the intent, dark face bent over him. He had tried to speak a moment before, but found he had no voice. His mouth was as dry as parchment, and someone was driving a new rail spur through his left side. He cleared his throat, concentrated mightily, and managed to croak, "Water, please."

The girl left his field of vision. He heard the clink of an earthen crock against a tin cup and tried to reach out with his right hand, but he was too weak. The hand simply did not respond to his command. Seeing this, the girl quickly leaned close and, looping one arm around his head, lifted it. With her other hand she rested the cup against his parched lips, then gently tipped it up.

He felt the cool, refreshing liquid move down his throat. It went too fast. He choked. The spasm caused the dull pain in his side to erupt with sharp virulence. For a moment it was almost unendurable. But, as his coughing subsided, so did the pain. The girl had pulled back to wait. When she saw he was ready again, she let him drink the full contents of the cup.

The girl sat back. Longarm turned his head to look at her.

"More," he told her.

She smiled and filled him a second cup. Afterward, his voice strong enough now, he asked, "Who in the hell are you, and where did you come from?"

"I am Running Moon. You are in Black Feather's cabin."

"Cabin?"

"Yes. My brother's. He is rancher and hunter. Like white man. He read Holy Bible, too. He is called Jack."

Longarm looked about the cabin. It impressed him with its roominess and its no-nonsense, masculine neatness. The gear was all hung up, the wooden floor swept, the huge fireplace uncluttered and clean of ash. Over the mantel were crossed several fine flintlocks polished to a gleaming finish. It looked no different from any other rancher's cabin he had found himself in over the years, just a mite better kept.

"How did I get here? Was it your brother found me?"

She sat back. "Running Moon save you. I see you fight those three, then try to mount your horse. So I bring you here."

"You? By yourself?"

She nodded, her dark eyes glowing proudly.

"Then I owe you my life, Running Moon."

She looked at him, her face darkening in embarrassment, then shrugged. "I do not want to see such a brave man die."

Longarm was deeply moved. He closed his eyes for a moment. When he reopened them, he said, "Where's your brother now?"

"He has gone back to the canyon where the three dead men are. He say it is foolish to let their guns rust and leave all that fine ammunition to the vultures."

"How long have I been here?"

"Four days."

"That long?"

Running Moon smiled and nodded. "Yes. For two days you toss and cry out. Many times we have to hold you down. This was not easy. You are very strong."

"I don't feel very strong—not now, anyway. Is my side clear of infection?"

Running Moon's face grew serious. "Black Feather and I keep your wound clean. We find mold for it, like Zuni medicine man teach. It is many days and still it does not smell. But you are cut bad inside. So you must lay still for long time before you ride again."

"Maybe," he said.

Looking down at his side, he saw the crude bandages. It felt sore, but was not too uncomfortable—until he reached down to feel it. The pain coming once again from deep inside was sudden and excruciating. Running Moon was right. He was still hurt bad inside.

Longarm took a deep breath and asked for more water. Gently, she lifted his head and rested the cup against his lower lip. He drank deep, gratefully, thanked her, then lay his head back down and plunged at once into a deep, dreamless sleep.

Jed Tomlinson watched the Ute Indian picking over the dead men. The Ute had brought with him a packhorse and a large aparejo into which he was packing the sixguns, rifles, and other weapons. Before long, the son of a bitch would probably begin picking gold out of their teeth. He was sure as hell doing a thorough job of it, and there was no doubt he had known from the start where to come. He had trailed down off the canyon rim straight to the bodies, chased away the vultures, and set to work.

Shifting patiently, Tomlinson waited for the Indian to finish. The Ute was dressed like any white man, faded Levi's, cotton shirt and vest, wide-brimmed Stetson. But he had the flat, polished face of an Indian, and he sure as hell moved like one. And, since he had known where to find these three, it could only have been the one who killed them—that goddamn deputy marshal—who had told him where to look.

Tomlinson shook his head in pure amazement that Longarm had managed to get away from those three. Each one of them was as cold-blooded a killer as he'd ever come across.

He had no love for any of them. Hardcases from the border, they had offered to kill the marshal for twenty bucks each man and had been glad to get the business. It must have been a mean, hardscrabble land that bred scorpions like them. And now there they were, laid out in the shadow of this canyon wall, being picked over by a redskin. That Longarm was sure as hell a tough hombre to bushwhack. And for the first time in his life, Tomlinson was no longer so all-fired certain he was going to come out of this adventure with all his parts intact.

The Ute grabbed his packhorse's lead and mounted up. As he disappeared beyond the rim a moment later, Tomlinson urged his mount out from the shadows of the canyon wall and took after him. It was close to dusk, and he was hoping the Ute would not keep going through the night. Tomlinson was not so good tracking in the dark, especially tracking a redskin.

He'd likely end up wearing a blade in his ribs.

Chapter 4

Longarm woke from a deep sleep with Running Moon bending over him. He tipped his head slightly and saw that she was naked.

"You are erect," she whispered.

Longarm smiled and glanced down at the sharp mound between his legs. Yes, he sure as hell was. He had been having trouble with his self-control most of the afternoon as he lay on his back watching Running Moon busy herself about the cabin. Now his impertinent organ had made pretty clear its intent, and Running Moon was answering its call.

"I did not think it would be good for you to . . . exert yourself," Running Moon explained as she lifted his blanket and eased onto the cot beside him. "But I see now you are in distress."

That was putting it mildly, Longarm told himself, reaching over to feel his side. The wound was still tender. But it was the guts beneath that he knew would protest most fiercely if he made any sustained, violent exertion. Yet the silken smoothness of Running Moon's thigh against his kindled a fire in his loins he could not deny.

She dropped one arm over his shoulder, kissed him with glowing lips, then let her hand drop onto his swollen erection. Gently, sweetly, she let her fingers play about it until she took a firm grip on it and began her gentle massage. More and more rapidly her hand pumped until, straining mightily, he lifted his thigh in sudden, urgent anticipation, disregarding the pain now erupting from deep under his rib cage.

An instant before he was about to let go, she slipped deftly backward and guided his engorged erection deep inside her, finishing him off with three quick, savage downstrokes. Despite the pain, he came in a violent, bucking explosion that caused Running Moon to cry out delightedly as she hung on. When at last he was spent, she lay forward on his chest and kissed him lightly about the face and neck.

"What about you?" he murmured.

"Next time," she told him softly, "maybe you will use your hand, too."

"That's a promise."

She laughed and kissed him lightly on his forehead, then slipped off the cot. He caught a glimpse of her sleek figure passing through a beam of moonlight on the way to her bedroom, then closed his eyes and slept.

Black Feather arrived late the next day. He was a powerful Indian almost as tall as Longarm with eyes that glinted like two chunks of basalt. His nose was hooked, his brows and chin chiseled from granite. Leading his packhorse, he left the timber that crowded the barn, a smile on his broad face when he saw the two of them sitting out on the porch.

Running Moon left her chair on a run to greet him. The Indian lifted his left foot over his saddlehorn and slipped off his horse just in time to catch her in his arms. With her leading the packhorse and he his paint, they continued on to the cabin as Longarm, leaning on his hickory branch, pushed himself erect and hobbled off the porch to greet Black Feather.

"You look well," Black Feather said, nodding approvingly. "Maybe soon you ride."

"Thanks to you and Running Moon."

Running Moon quickly introduced the two.

"How much did you get, Black Feather?" Longarm asked, indicating the bulging aparejos tied to his packhorse.

Black Feather smiled broadly. "Many weapons." Reaching into the nearest aparejo, he pulled forth a bowie knife and held it out to Longarm. "Your blood is still on this blade," he told Longarm. "Take it. It is fine weapon."

Longarm almost winced as he hefted the big bowie. It was at least fifteen inches long. No wonder his insides still protested whenever he took a deep breath. He handed it back to Black Feather.

"Take it, Jack. You earned it."

Taking it back gratefully, Black Feather ran his fingers over the blade for an instant before turning to the rest of his loot. He had brought back three Winchesters and Colts, the gunbelts, and several other knives, as well as the bridles and reins from the outlaws' horses. Black Feather didn't take the horses, Longarm figured, because they could be recognized by white men who might have known the riders—and nothing inspires a crowd of white men faster than an Indian horse thief.

While Running Moon led the horses over to the barn, Black Feather and Longarm turned and headed for the cabin. They were sitting at the kitchen table drinking coffee when she rejoined them a few minutes later. It was near sundown and Running Moon started to heat up the venison stew she had prepared earlier for supper. As the aroma of the hot stew filled the kitchen, Longarm's stomach began churning in happy anticipation.

"Jack," Longarm asked, leaning back in his chair, "what do you know about any gold strikes or mines in the area?"

"There is no gold in these mountains."

"You sure of that?"

"I am sure."

"Are there any Chinese around here?" Longarm asked.

"Over next pass. Many Chinese. They are left from time when they come to dig for silver. When mines shut down, they stay. Now they live in valley."

"You think maybe those Chinese might've struck gold?"

"No gold," Black Feather insisted, shaking his head.

Running Moon turned away from the stove to face them. "When we were in Green's Creek two weeks ago, I hear talk, crazy talk, maybe—but some say the Chinese have found . . ." She frowned, groping for the word. ". . . mother lode, I think."

"That means it would be quite a strike," Longarm told her. "The mother lode would be the vein where all the gold they panned from the streams was coming from."

Black Feather looked sharply at his sister. "When you hear this?"

"When I wait outside general store with horses. I hear some men speak of this. They sit on bench outside the store and talk very loud. I try not to listen, but I cannot help it."

The Indian shrugged and looked back at Longarm. "I did not hear such talk. I was too busy. But I know for sure the mines around Green's Creek are played out." He shrugged. "So now maybe the white men dream of new strike."

"That's all you know?"

"More I do not want to know. When white men smell

gold, he go crazy, like Indian who drink too much whiskey."

The conversation ended there as Running Moon began serving the stew she had spent the day preparing.

Hell, this was working out just fine, Tomlinson reminded himself as he stole closer to the darkened cabin. It was past midnight and the lamps had been blown out long before. With this crazy bulldog of a U. S. marshal out of the way, he would be able to breathe easy once more.

Not wishing to disturb the horses in the barn, Tomlinson came at the cabin from the rear. There was an aspen tree between him and the cabin. He reached it, ducked low, and crept closer to the rear of the cabin. Looking in through a window, he was impressed by how much the interior resembled that of a white man's cabin. But that didn't fool him. This fellow he'd trailed here was a redskin clear to his liver. Tomlinson shook his head in disgust. He didn't have any respect for a man who'd turn his back on his own kind.

He moved along the wall, came to the corner, turned it, and headed for the next window to give himself a better view of the cabin's layout. Peering in through the cabin's side window, he saw two bedrooms on the far end of the cabin—and a cot in the near corner. He chuckled. There were two on that cot, and they sure as hell weren't sleeping.

All he would have to do was bust in through that front door, his gun blazing. By the time he took care of the two, he'd be ready for the Ute sleeping in one of them bedrooms. Serve the bastard right. He should've kept a closer tether on his woman.

Tomlinson ducked away from the window and moved around to the front of the cabin. Despite the bravado he had been pumping into himself all evening, his palms were sweaty as he approached the door. He held back for a moment and took a deep breath. He knew he was going against a man who had already accounted for Sharlow, Grunewald, and those three gunslicks.

Marshal Custis Long was one tough hombre to bring down.

Tomlinson wiped off his palm on his Levi's, unholstered his Colt, and cocked it. Then he stepped carefully up onto the porch and placed his palm against the door.

The moment Longarm caught the shadow at the window, he rolled off Running Moon, his big hand held firmly but gently over her mouth. She was startled at first, and perhaps even a little angry at him for stopping so abruptly. But when she saw the sudden concern in his narrowed eyes, she realized they were in danger. Relaxing immediately, she waited for Longarm to take his hand away from her mouth.

When he did, he leaned close and whispered, "Someone's out there. We got a visitor."

At once she slipped from the cot and darted on silent feet to her brother's bedroom. Grunting painfully, Longarm reached up for his gunbelt hanging from a nail. Removing the Colt from his holster, he hefted it to test its load, then turned to face the door. It was Tomlinson out there, he was willing to bet. The son of a bitch must have followed Black Feather here.

Longarm heard a slight sound in Black Feather's bedroom doorway. Glancing over, he saw the Ute crouching in the open doorway, a big blade gleaming in his hand. As Longarm heard the soft, barely perceptible creak of a porch plank, he glanced quickly back at the door.

The crazy redhead was coming in through the front door, gun blazing.

Longarm dropped to the floor and, grunting painfully, rolled swiftly away from the cot, coming to rest in the corner beside the wood stove. He had just pulled up his Colt when the door burst open. His gun thundering, Tomlinson stood in the doorway pouring slugs into Longarm's cot. Then he spun to face the bedrooms, sending a withering fire at both doorways.

Longarm fired back, the Colt kicking in his hand with an unfamiliar heaviness, the recoil tearing at his side. He saw the startled Tomlinson stagger back momentarily, then swing his Colt back around. Longarm fired a second time and heard the slug bite into the doorjamb beside Tomlinson, who fired back at him. The round whanged off the stove and exploded through the window behind Longarm. Again Longarm fired. Tomlinson buckled over slightly, then vanished from the doorway.

Pulling himself erect, Longarm limped swiftly to the door. He saw a shadowy figure disappearing behind a large boulder. A moment later came the swift drumming of Tomlinson's horse.

Son of a bitch! Longarm was sure he'd caught the bastard twice.

"Longarm!" Running Moon cried.

Longarm turned around to see Running Moon trying to hold up Black Feather. The Indian must have caught one of Tomlinson's slugs. Running Moon and Longarm helped Black Feather back into his bedroom. Running Moon lit a lamp and Longarm examined the wound.

One of Tomlinson's rounds had caught the Indian in the right chest, smashing through a rib and up into his lung. Already a thin trickle of blood was oozing from a corner of his mouth.

Unless Black Feather could be taken to a surgeon for removal of the bullet, the wound would most likely be fatal. Already Black Feather had lost consciousness and a sick pallor had lightened his bronzed features.

"The white doctor!" Running Moon cried. "We must take Black Feather to him!"

"Where is he?"

"He live in Green's Creek."

"Do you have a buggy?"

"Yes. We have buckboard."

"Harness the horses to it, then come back here and help me get your brother into it. We should make the valley by morning."

With a quick nod, Running Moon hurried from the cabin.

Dawn was breaking when they reached a canyon west of Maria. As they entered it, Longarm heard the sound of shoes on stone above and behind him. Turning on the wagon seat, he saw a ring of horsemen closing in on them. Its leader was Malcolm Hartridge.

With a gunbelt strapped about his paunch, he looked a lot less uncertain than he had in Green's Creek. He was wearing a large black floppy-brimmed hat to keep the sun off his face and neck. The string tie at his throat was as grimy as his frock coat. The man had been doing some riding, it seemed.

Longarm hauled back on the team's reins as the riders overtook and surrounded the wagon. Hartridge pulled to a halt beside Longarm. His smile was cold.

"What's this, Marshal? What're you doin' with a Ute squaw?"

"And her brother," Longarm told him, indicating Black Feather behind him. "He's wounded. We're taking him in to Green's Creek to see the doctor."

"That so?"

"Far from home, ain't you, Hartridge?" Longarm asked.

"I have a mine up here I'm running," he explained.

"And you need this many men, do you?"

"You got any idea how many crazy prospectors we got in these hills? They're as hard to stomp out as cockroaches.

You saw how hard it was to get that redhead in Green's Creek. And there's others like him."

"They're after your silver, are they?"

"What else would they be after?"

"Gold."

"They ain't no gold left in these hills, Marshal," Hartridge told him.

Longarm nodded, then gathered up the reins and prepared to release the brake. "We'll be moving on, Hartridge. I want to get this fellow to a doctor."

Hartridge peered into the wagon and studied Black Feather for a moment. Then he looked at Longarm. "This fellow's a Ute. I know him. Black Feather."

"Right."

"He's wanted."

"For what?"

"Horse stealing and claim jumping. He don't need to go anywhere, Long. You can leave him right here with us. If he ain't dead by sundown, we'll string him up for you. And that's a promise."

"You got proof of those charges, Hartridge?"

"I don't need any. My word's worth a sight more than any damned savage."

Longarm turned to Running Moon. "What about those charges?"

"This man speak lies, Longarm."

Longarm turned back to Hartridge. "That's good enough for me, Hartridge," he snapped. "Get your men out of my way."

Hartridge laughed. "And what makes you think you're goin' anywhere? Any man who gives aid and comfort to escaped fugitives don't get to tell me and my men what to do."

Dropping the reins, Longarm reached across his belt for

his Colt, but before he could draw it, he heard the sound of sixguns cocking all around him. His hand freezing on his .44's grips, Longarm peered up at Hartridge with unbridled fury. "Let us go, Hartridge. You got no quarrel with us."

"Forget it, Marshal. You ain't goin' nowhere." He reached out a hand. "Now maybe you better let me have that gun. Just lift it out nice and easy."

Reluctantly, Longarm gave Hartridge his Colt.

"Now you come with us," Hartridge ordered.

"Where in hell you taking us?"

"To that silver mine I told you about. It ain't far from here."

"Damn your eyes, Hartridge! I told you. This here Indian's got to see a doctor!"

"And I'm tellin' you he ain't seein' none! Ain't you heard? The only good Injun's a dead one."

"If he dies, Hartridge, I'll bring you in," Longarm warned.

"For what?"

"Murder."

Hartridge laughed. "You must be out of your head. When a white man kills a redskin, that's not murder, that's a public service. Where in hell were you brought up, Long?"

Before Longarm could say or do anything more, a rider reached over and took one of their team's horses by the bridle and pulled it around. A moment later Longarm was driving the team up a steep slope following a deeply rutted road, with Hartridge's hired guns riding so close, Longarm could smell their rancid sweat.

He reached over with one hand to comfort Running Moon. He didn't dare look back at the unconscious Black Feather. The Ute's only hope now, Longarm reckoned angrily, was to die before this madman Hartridge strung him up.

• • •

It took until noon to reach the silver mine. It was in a narrow canyon. Upon the canyon floor, close about the mine entrance, ten or fifteen flimsily constructed cabins and buildings had been erected, with the shaft head and holding bins perched precariously on long stilts as they extended out from the side of one mountain wall. A pall of rock dust hung over the valley, and Longarm had to blink to keep the wind-borne grit out of his eyes. High-sided ore wagons drawn by teams of gaunt Percherons stood under the holding bins. The sound of ore cascading down the chutes resounded heavily in the air.

To Longarm's surprise, except for a few engineers and overseers, everywhere he looked he saw Chinese coolies dressed raggedly in their traditional black pajama-like garments, every one of them looking pathetically emaciated. Not until he rode close enough to view them individually did he notice the cruel chains hobbling their feet.

Longarm turned to Running Moon. "You ever been here before?"

She shook her head.

"Did you know about this mine?" he asked.

"I hear talk of it sometime. Black Feather tell me to keep away from here. He say some women are taken by these men."

Hartridge had ridden ahead to confer with one of his overseers. He rode back now toward the buggy, raising his arm for Longarm to halt. Longarm reined in his horses as Hartridge pulled up beside him.

"Here we are, Long. Your new place of employment."

"What the hell are you saying, Hartridge?"

"You heard me," Hartridge replied. "These here yellow bastards need a white man to work aside them. You might say it gives them a model to follow."

Longarm felt outrage, then disbelief—until he looked

into the man's eyes and saw in them nothing but cold, unblinking calculation. He thought of Jed Tomlinson.

"You in this with Tomlinson?" he asked.

Hartridge laughed easily. "Hell, Jed's just a crazy man ramming about these mountains. I promise you, if I get hold of him, I'll just send him down into the shaft with you." He smiled broadly. "That would make for some real interesting fireworks, I'm thinking."

"Especially with all that dynamite," said another rider as he pulled to a halt beside Hartridge.

Hartridge turned to the newcomer. "I got you another strong back, Pincherman," Hartridge said. Then he looked back at Longarm. "This here's Charles Pincherman, my mine superintendent. From now on, you'll answer to him."

Pincherman smiled as he contemplated Longarm. The superintendent was a cadaverous fellow with the stink of bad whiskey and old vomit hanging about him like a cloud. His thinning hair was prematurely gray, his eyes red-rimmed and furtive. He was dressed in a dust-laden but well tailored suit. The celluloid collar he wore hung open, however, and his string tie was carelessly knotted.

"I'm a deputy U. S. marshal, Hartridge," Longarm reminded him. "If I don't show up pretty soon, there's going to be others coming after me."

"Let 'em come," said Hartridge. "We can always use a few more strong backs."

Pincherman laughed, then spoke with sudden, flat insolence at Longarm. "Get down off that seat, Mr. Deputy Marshal. I'll show you to your quarters. You're too late for today's shift, but don't worry none. You'll start soon enough."

"Like hell I will."

Pincherman pulled a bullwhip out of his belt and swung its handle like a club, catching Longarm in the back of the head and pitching him headlong. As Longarm sprawled in the dust, he glanced back and saw another rider jump onto the buggy seat beside Running Moon and snatch up the reins. In angry futility Longarm watched the wagon being driven off, the badly wounded Black Feather still unconscious in the bed of the wagon. The last thing he glimpsed was Running Moon looking back at him in dismay.

"Get up," Pincherman told Longarm, "and follow me."

Longarm's knife wound was still not completely healed; the moment he struck the ground, the pain had erupted in his side with renewed vigor. But he was beyond the control of reason by this time. Leaping to his feet, he reached up and grabbed Pincherman about the waist, stepped back, and flung him viciously to the ground.

Pincherman struck hard, the back of his head slamming down upon the unyielding ground. As he raised himself to his hands and knees and tried to shake the cobwebs from his befuddled senses, Longarm kicked him in the chops, then reached down for the bullwhip the superintendent had dropped and managed to get in a couple of powerful licks before Hartridge's men could leap down from their horses and pull him off. They pinned Longarm's arms behind him and held him steady.

Eyes wild with fury, a large red stripe on his face and another on his neck, Pincherman flung himself erect, then lunged at Longarm. But his fury made him almost impotent as his pale fists beat at the big lawman futilely about the chest and shoulders. At length he recovered his senses enough to snatch up his bullwhip. Uncoiling it, he stepped back.

"Let the son of a bitch loose!" he told his men.

They stepped back from Longarm as the mine superintendent began wielding his whip with cold, deadly accuracy. Soon he had Longarm's shirt front in strips as he flailed the flesh on Longarm's chest into broad, puckering stripes. Only when Longarm had collapsed to the ground, his head down, did Pincherman, exhausted by his nearly demented fury, finally run out of steam and pull back, panting.

Longarm lifted his head. The sky spun sickeningly as he tried to get to his feet. Then he felt himself being hauled roughly erect, after which he was dragged toward a line of miserable shacks and flung at last into one long room filled with army cots. As he crashed to the floor, he heard the door slam shut behind him, and a bolt was thrown.

It took him a while to get his bearings. When he did, he sat up and looked about him. He was the only one in the room. He searched his torn vest for his watch and the derringer. The face of the watch was broken, but the derringer was intact, both chambers loaded. Ignoring the fresh surge of pain that rocketed up his left side whenever he moved, he located a loose board in the flooring near a corner. Lifting it, he managed to hide the watch and derringer under it.

Only then did he allow himself to pass out.

Chapter 5

Longarm was awake when they came for him later that same afternoon—two men, one of them carrying a rubber truncheon, the other keeping his hand close about the butt of his Colt.

Longarm had seen them through the window and waited for them lying face down on a cot. Keeping perfectly still until the two men reached his cot, he lashed out suddenly, catching the fellow with the truncheon in the face with the back of his forearm. As the guard reeled back, both hands held up to his smashed face, he dropped his truncheon. Snatching it up, Longarm caught the second man on the side of the head with it, slamming him backward over a cot.

But he came up fast, tugging his Colt free of its holster.

Bringing the truncheon down on him again, Longarm smashed the gun from his hand. The Colt struck the floor and skittered away under the cots. As the guard reeled back holding his wrist, Longarm flailed away at him with the truncheon, catching him about the head and shoulders until he caught him on the side of his head, snapping it back with sickening force. The guard collapsed loosely to the floor in front of Longarm.

But by this time the racket had drawn more guards. As Longarm started for the doorway, he found it blocked by two men. Putting his head down, he rushed them, knocking one back, but not the other. There was a brief, violent struggle before the truncheon was taken from him. Not long after that Longarm was on the floor once more, beaten senseless.

It was late the same day when he awoke. The barracks were still empty except for him. The first thing he saw clearly was the tear-stained face of Running Moon as she gazed down at him. She had been swabbing his face with a damp cloth.

Behind her stood Hartridge. He was holding a riding crop. Beyond him were more of the mine operator's grim henchmen. Pincherman, his face swollen, his eyes bright with suppressed rage, stood at Hartridge's elbow.

"You see, Long," Hartridge said as soon as he saw Longarm's eyes open. "We ain't savages. We brought your Indian squaw to bathe your bloody brow."

Longarm reached up and took Running Moon's hand gently in his and guided her to one side, so he could have a clearer look at Hartridge and the others. "What're you up to, you bastard?"

Hartridge turned to someone waiting in the open doorway. The fellow nodded quickly and vanished. Hartridge turned back to Longarm.

"Get to your feet—if you can," Hartridge told the lawman.

Longarm swung his legs over the cot. They were shackled, but he managed to stand up, the pain in his side causing him to wince in spite of himself.

"Fine," said Hartridge. "Now, if you please, Mr. Deputy U. S. Marshal, just step over here to the window. I want you to see firsthand the meaning of frontier justice, so you'll know we mean what we say."

As Longarm moved carefully around the cots to reach the window, Running Moon hung back. Hartridge noticed this. "I suggest you join your protector," he told her sharply. "This is for your benefit as well."

Beside him, Pincherman snickered.

Longarm felt Running Moon come close up to him as he halted in front of the window and looked out. He saw some of Hartridge's men crowding about the loading platform in front of a long shed. As Longarm watched, a rope was dropped from a second-story window to a couple of men standing on the platform.

In that instant, Longarm knew what he had been revived to witness.

He reached out quickly and took Running Moon's hand, squeezing it so hard she winced. "Don't look," he told her.

She looked wide-eyed up at Longarm, then back out across the yard.

At that moment a horse-drawn wagon pulled to a halt in front of the platform. Someone jumped into the wagon bed and thrust the still figure of Black Feather upright as another dropped the noose around his neck.

Another one struck the rump of the horse with a whip. The fellow on the wagon jumped to the ground as the wagon lurched forward. Black Feather's body toppled off the rear of the wagon and plunged down to halt abruptly as the rope halted his descent. He swung back and forth for a moment, then began to twist slowly, the evening sun lighting clearly his unnaturally twisted neck and the wide, bulging eyes.

Longarm ducked his head away from the sight. Running Moon's head was bowed, tears streaming down her face. She had not uttered a sound, but he knew she had just died inside. He looked at Hartridge and his henchmen and knew that he would live to make them pay.

But at the moment he felt only a deep weariness. There seemed no folly, no vice, no cruelty some men could not commit . . . and with a smile, more often than not. They were members of the Devil's own legion, and for every one of them he or any other lawman brought to justice, two more leaped up to take his place. And now, it seemed, a crack regiment of that hellish army stood around him and Running Moon.

Longarm reached out to comfort Running Moon. She buried her face in his chest, her shoulders shaking gently.

Pincherman grabbed Running Moon and pulled her roughly away from Longarm. He yanked her across the room to the doorway, then flung her into one of the guards' arms. In a fury, Longarm lunged for the man, but another of the guards simply thrust his truncheon down between Longarm's chains. Longarm went sprawling.

"Forget the heroics, Mr. Deputy," Hartridge said, smiling coldly down at Longarm. "You haven't got a chance. There's no use fighting back. There's too many of us and too little of you."

Longarm got cautiously to his feet, using one of the cots for support.

Smiling, Hartridge rested his riding crop against the side of Longarm's chin. "Think of your squaw, Longarm. Do you doubt we can do anything we want with her?"

Longarm said nothing.

"Tomorrow morning, if you go off to work like a good boy, I promise we will let Running Moon sleep in her own bed. Until then, she will comfort our beds. I'm sure she'll protest. She is almost as stubborn as you. But I don't think there is any doubt who will prevail in the end. Do you get my meaning, Marshal?"

"Leave her alone. I'll give you no more trouble."

"But how can we trust you? You are a very stubborn man. Tonight we will just have to give you another example of our resolve. It will be an instructive lesson, I am sure." He tapped Longarm gently on the side of the head with his riding crop. "And you are a man who needs such lessons, I am afraid."

"Keep your filthy hands off her!"

"No," Hartridge said. "We can't do that. I told you, I must be allowed to make my point." He smiled. "You see? I can be just as willful and stubborn as you."

"You bastard. I'll kill you."

"Ah, but you can't! You are no longer a lawman. Now you are just one of many who labor in the bowels of the earth. You have been toppled from your high estate. Now, perhaps, you will learn what it is like to grovel before your master. It will be a humbling experience, I am afraid. But you know what they say—humility is good for the soul."

Longarm reached out suddenly and grabbed Hartridge's riding crop. Twisting it out of his hand, he lashed out, catching Hartridge flush on the cheekbone. Yelping in pain, Hartridge reeled back. Two of his men flung themselves on Longarm and attempted to twist the crop from his hand. Longarm struggled furiously against their superior weight until he heard Running Moon's scream.

He gave up struggling at once. The two men dumped him unceremoniously to the floor and proceeded to leave the room. Watching from the floor, Longarm saw Pincherman and Hartridge dragging the helpless Running Moon out through the doorway.

• • •

On his cot near midnight, Longarm came awake with cold sweat standing out on his forehead. A woman's screams—Running Moon's—had awakened him. Sitting up, he saw a dark grouping of heads and shoulders at the moonlit window as his fellow prisoners peered out across the yard toward the overseer's quarters. The scream came again, sharper, more piercing.

He flung himself off the cot and rushed to the window, almost tripping over his chains. A grizzled old-timer turned at his approach and ducked out of his way to give him a place at the window. Another fellow, a Mexican, glanced at him, his dark, liquid eyes glowing with anger.

"That's your woman, is it?" he said. "I was hopin' you'd sleep through it."

When the next scream came, Longarm shuddered visibly.

"Look!" a third white man standing behind Longarm cried, pointing.

A sudden rectangle of light had exploded onto the darkness as someone broke from the building and began running across the yard toward them. Three men rushed out after the running figure. Longarm drew in his breath as he recognized the slim, naked form of Running Moon approaching their barracks. With discouraging swiftness, the three men overtook the girl. There was a sudden, vicious struggle. Longarm saw the three men's arms rising and falling as they beat her into submission. After a painfully long interval, the largest of the three slung her unconscious form over his back and carried her back to the building.

Standing in the doorway, waiting, was Pincherman, his slight figure clearly outlined in the light. As the three men neared him with their frail burden, he called out something and was answered with a brutal bark of laughter. A moment later the door closed on them. Darkness fell once more over the yard.

Seething, not thinking clearly at all, Longarm pulled

away from the window and hobbled over to the door. It was a frail, rotting barrier, and he lowered his shoulder and ran at it repeatedly. When it did not give, he turned to the room full of men. They were standing by their cots watching him intently, begrimed miners, Chinese coolies mostly, in addition to three white men, looking equally grimy.

"Give me a hand!" Longarm demanded. "We'll break it down!"

"Take it easy, mister," said one of them, an old-timer.

Furious at their lack of support, Longarm turned back to the door. Ignoring the waves of pain still coursing up his left side, he put down his shoulder and rushed at it as hard as he could with his feet shackled. The door gave slightly, and from the other side came a sharp order.

A rifle and a sixgun barked. Bullets slammed through the door, narrowly missing Longarm. As he ducked quickly aside, three more volleys followed, the rounds slamming into the wall behind him. One round ricocheted off a cot's iron frame. In the silence that followed, Longarm heard laughter from the two guards on the porch.

Longarm moved wearily back to his cot and slumped down onto it. He had been acting irrationally since his capture, he realized. And this last outburst had been the most foolish. Glancing around him at the pale, indistinct faces staring somberly at him, he felt a sudden shame. He would get nowhere like this, and these men knew it. He would have to bide his time, wait and watch for his opportunity. He still had his derringer. He must calm down.

He realized then that he no longer cared about Jed Tomlinson. He was beyond that now. All he wanted from this moment on was to bring down—by fair means or foul—Hartridge and Pincherman. No matter how long it took, he would make those two pay for this night.

• • •

In the weeks that followed, Longarm presented a much more docile picture to his captors. Meanwhile, he got to know the three other white prisoners.

Charlie Fiddle was the oldest of the three. A grizzled, white-haired man in his sixties, at least, he was a bent but unbroken veteran of the West with clear eyes and almost all of his teeth. He had been prospecting in the mountains northwest of Denver when he heard reports of a gold strike being worked by Chinese coolies. He had heard also of a fabulous town that had grown up around this strike, one that was gradually coming to resemble those Chinese villages in the Pearl River delta in Canton, China, the place from which most of the coolies had come.

Certain he would be able to outsmart the foolish orientals who had stumbled on the gold, Charlie had set out to find it, but had lost his way in the mountains and come upon this silver mine. Pincherman had greeted him cordially enough at first, feeding him handsomely. But the next day Charlie Fiddle found chains fastened to his ankles, and he was sent into the mine to work alongside the Chinese coolies.

The other two men told essentially the same story. Burt Robbins—a young man in his twenties with a straggly, reddish mustache and big, sleepy brown eyes—had been sitting on the hotel porch in Green's Creek when he heard talk of a fabulous gold strike by some Chinese coolies who years before had been driven from most of the silver and gold mines in the area. Not long after, he set out to find this strike himself. Hartridge's men came on him struggling through a narrow canyon and brought him in forcefully, as they had Longarm.

Sanchez, a Mexican, had been on his way to California, doing his best to outdistance the sheriff of a small border town in Texas, when he was caught in Pincherman's net and put to work alongside Charlie Fiddle and Burt Robbins.

Of the three, Sanchez was the toughest and best-conditioned. Almost as tall as Longarm, he had a heavy shock of blue-black hair, powerful, jutting black eyebrows, and eyes that gleamed coldly out of his swarthy face. His torso was a map of puckered scars from countless knife wounds, which he explained by saying he preferred a knife to a handgun.

In the mine, Sanchez worked naked, with only a towel around his crotch. He was oblivious to the awful heat, it seemed, his body glistening with sweat, his pick seldom slowing as he dug large chunks of the gray ore out of the veins and flung them into the rusted ore cart beside him.

The Chinese laboring nearby in the same drift seemed awed by Sanchez's energy and did their best to keep up, while Charlie Fiddle was content to pick dispiritedly at the ore. Burt contented himself with an occasional flurry of activity, his outbursts generated as much by frustration as anything else.

Working alongside these three, Longarm labored steadily, making no effort to outdo Sanchez, content simply to keep a steady pace. And, before long, he felt his strength gradually returning.

After the first day a small, wiry Chinaman of indefinable age joined the four of them, keeping closest to Longarm, as if he found in the big lawman's size and steady productivity a protective armor. When asked his name, he only nodded agreeably and pointed to his chin. So they called him Chin. At first the three men, and Longarm as well, wondered if Chin might not be one of Pincherman's informants, but that fear gradually subsided, and within a week the Chinaman was allowed to drag his own cot to the far corner of the room where the four men slept.

They were working a main drift which ran from north to south along the line of the lode at a depth that was close to fifteen hundred feet. Narrow-gauge tracks on the floor of the drift had been laid for the cars that took the ore to the hoisting cages. Candles and lamps burned everywhere, and were kept going twenty-four hours a day. The temperature at this depth was over one hundred degrees, forcing Longarm and the others to wear breechclouts or long underwear. Many of the Chinamen, however, wore nothing but caps to keep the dirt out of their hair, and shoes to prevent the sharp quartz from digging into their feet.

There were days when their picks unearthed hot geysers which promptly filled the air with steam, causing the temperature to rise incredibly, turning the drift into a Turkish bath. Yet the men were forced to work through this without letup and, as a result, they consumed enormous quantities of water. Still, no matter how much they drank, it was never enough, and at the end of their shifts they returned to the surface gratefully, greeting the night sky as a benediction while they stood for a moment to let the cool mountain breeze caress their aching bodies.

By the third week Longarm was more than ready to make his break. One Sunday night, as the coolies settled into sleep, he woke Charlie Fiddle and the others. They gathered in a tight knot in the corner under an open window.

"What is it?" grumbled Charlies Fiddle, the last of the four men Longarm aroused.

"We're gettin' out of here," said Burt eagerly.

"What's that?"

"Just listen, old man," Sanchez hissed.

Chin took a deep breath and looked around at the sleeping men. They remained undisturbed. Some were snoring so loudly they could be heard above the steady thumping of the hoisting engines.

"That's right," said Longarm. "Keep it down. No sense in advertising what we're up to."

"So let's have it," said Burt. "When do we make our move?"

"Tomorrow night, about this time, I figure."

"What makes you think you can get out of here?" Sanchez asked. "You don' have so much luck the last time, I think."

"I have a weapon."

The three men glanced quickly at each other, then back at Longarm. "What kind of weapon?" asked Charlie.

"A derringer."

Sanchez snorted in derision. "Such a weapon is a toy! Maybe you think you can scare these fellows to death with it, hey?"

"Listen to my plan," Longarm snapped, "then say what you want. But listen first. Otherwise go back to sleep."

Sanchez shrugged quickly. "So, okay. I listen."

"Tomorrow night we have a scuffle just inside the door. We'll make enough noise so the two guards will come in to investigate. When they do, I'll cover them with the derringer. You three disarm them and tie them up. That'll give us a few more weapons."

"What then?" Burt asked.

"We take their keys and unchain the rest of the Chinamen and send them out. While Pincherman's busy rounding up his entire work force, we slip out."

"We'll need horses," said Charlie.

"Should be no problem. There's plenty in that stable across the yard."

"It won't be easy," said Burt.

"I'm game," said Sanchez immediately. "This hombre, he don' rot in this mine no longer." He looked at Longarm. "Where's this toy gun you got?"

Longarm smiled. "I'll get it when we need it."

Burt shrugged. "Suits me."

"There's just one more thing," Longarm told them, his

voice low now and intent. "We're not leaving here without Running Moon."

The men exchanged sudden glances.

"Hey, now listen, Long," Burt said. "We don't even know where they're keepin' her."

"Burt's right," said Charlie. "She's liable to slow us up somethin' fierce. We'll never make it with her in tow."

Longarm looked at Sanchez. "That how you feel?"

Sanchez shrugged. "I figure you got the gun. So I think we do what you say. It won't be so easy, though."

"I didn't think it would be. We'll find out tomorrow where they're keeping her." Longarm looked at the others. "If Running Moon doesn't come with us, we don't go anywhere. Understood?"

The men shrugged.

"Good." Longarm turned to Chin. "Chin, at breakfast you tell your people in the mess hall to find out where they are keeping the Indian girl. Tell them you want to know by the time we end our shift and head for the cookshack for supper."

"I tell them, yes," Chin said, nodding his head quickly, his teeth flashing in a grin. "You no worry. They find out. You see!"

"And one more thing, Chin. Don't tell any of your friends what we're planning."

Chin bobbed his head eagerly. "Chin no tell."

"All right," Longarm said, leaning back and looking about at the others. "That's it then. Now let's get some shuteye. And we better not work too hard tomorrow. Better we conserve our energy. We sure as hell will need it."

As the men dropped off to sleep, Longarm remained awake, staring at the ceiling, going over in his mind what he planned for the next day. He was aware that Sanchez was perfectly correct when he pointed out that Longarm's small derringer was not much of a match for the firepower Pincherman and his hirelings could command. To be successful, the plan would have to go off without a single slip-up—or Billy Vail would never know what had happened to his favorite deputy U. S. marshal.

On their way into the barracks the next evening, Chin overtook Longarm. In his eagerness to do so, he fell twice as his hobbled ankles got caught up by his chains.

Longarm bent his head for the information.

"Indian girl, she in long building over there," Chin said, indicating with a quick nod of his head the last building in the canyon. It was, Longarm knew, the general store and saloon where Pincherman's men hung out. "She on second floor with other Chinese women."

Longarm didn't have to be told what she was doing in that part of the camp. He nodded to the old Chinaman and followed him into the barracks. Once inside, he flung himself down on his cot.

The silver ore in this mine was a bluish-gray, oozing mass that hung from the ceilings and sometimes even between the timbers, at times falling at their feet in great, heavy masses. Though they had done all they could to slow their pace this day, the steam and the heat and the crumbling chunks of ore had kept them busy from the moment they reached the drift. They had been forced to work in ankle-deep water, and some of the rocks and pieces of shale they were forced to lift were so hot they scorched their hands. Despite rest periods every half-hour or so and all the water they could drink, it had been one of their worst days.

At first the men were too excited to sleep, but before long sleep claimed them. Before they passed out, Longarm assured them he would let them know when it was time. Chin was the last to fall asleep, and he did so with his face turned to Longarm. Watching him, Longarm had difficulty figuring out whether the old Chinaman's eyes were open or closed.

He watched Chin for a long time, and he still could not tell. At last he rolled over and slept. A little before midnight he came awake, every nerve in his body alert. It was time, he realized. He turned back around on his cot. Chin was sitting up on his cot, watching him.

Longarm nodded to him.

Chin leaned slightly forward. His voice barely audible, he whispered, "We go now?"

Longarm shook his head, lay back down, and rolled over once again, pulling his blanket up over his shoulder and closing his eyes. In a few minutes he was fast asleep.

Hours later, Longarm was awakened by the sudden harsh tramp of boots on the barracks floor. He sat up quickly. A heavy hand caught him on the shoulders and forced him back down onto the cot. A lantern flared suddenly above him.

Pincherman and his favorite henchman—a thin, pale runt called Jody—were standing beside Longarm's cot. Other guards were posted in the open doorway. What interested Longarm was that both Jody and Pincherman were carrying double-barreled shotguns and had strapped sixguns to their hips.

"What's the matter, Pincherman? Can't you sleep?"

Pincherman frowned, then stepped closer. He peered for a long moment down at Longarm, then turned to Jody.

"Search the son of a bitch."

The search was thorough and before it was over, Longarm had no doubt at all what they were looking for—his derringer. Finished with the frisk, Jody looked back at Pincherman and shrugged.

"It ain't on him," he said.

"Why don't you tell me what you're lookin' for?" Longarm inquired. "Maybe I could help."

Without replying, Pincherman looked quickly around the room, then back at Jody. "It must be in here somewhere. Find it."

"If you're looking for a derringer," Longarm spoke up, "you won't find it."

Pincherman's eyes narrowed. He stepped closer. "What'd you do with it?"

"That's simple. I never had one."

"How's that?"

"I just wanted to find out if Chin really was your informant."

"Chin?"

"That's right—that little rat behind you—the one you hired to keep an eye on us. I fed him a story about us making a break with my trusty derringer. He went for it. So did you, it seems."

Pincherman flung about and cuffed Chin to the floor. Then he kicked him. Squealing like a stuck pig, Chin began crawling from the place on his hands and knees, while the rest of Pincherman's men hastened him on his way with well-timed shots in the ass.

Looking back at Longarm, Pincherman said, "You say that was just a story, huh?"

"It did the trick."

"Yes, it did, you son of a bitch. And it kept me up all night."

"That really breaks my heart," Longarm told him.

"And I'll break your back. Tomorrow you'll do two consecutive shifts."

As he said this, he unholstered his gun and swung the barrel around sharply, catching Longarm on the side of his head. As Longarm went flying backward onto his cot, Pincherman and his lieutenant spun about and stalked from the place.

The door slammed shut behind them. Longarm heard the bolt being rammed home and the key turning in the padlock. A moment later they heard the sound of Pincherman and the others tramping off the porch.

Longarm sat up groggily, holding his head together with both hands.

"Jesus Christ," whispered Burt, hurrying over to Longarm's cot. "You mean you suspected Chin all this time?"

"No. Just tonight."

"What'd he do?"

"I'm not sure I know. But there was something—it was in his eyes."

Sanchez slapped Longarm on the back. "That's quick thinkin', *amigo*. We owe you our lives, maybe."

"Maybe," Longarm agreed.

"What do you think they'll do to Chin?" Burt asked.

"Don't you know?"

"Yeah," said Charlie Fiddle. "I guess we do know, at that. Once they caught four of them beggars tryin' to escape. They stripped them and hung them up on meat hooks. Kept them hanging there till they got real ripe. If they meant it for a lesson, it worked. These here coolies haven't tried an escape since."

"That poor son of a bitch," said Burt softly.

Sanchez snorted. "Hey, listen, *amigo*. This one will not be sorry to see Chin hangin' from meat hook. Pincherman and that little bastard were waiting out there for us tonight. As soon as we step out onto that porch, we would have been blasted."

Longarm nodded. That was the way he had it figured, too. It would have been another object lesson for the coolies. Longarm lay back down and closed his eyes. They weren't going anywhere this night after all, it seemed, and he would need his sleep for that double shift Pincherman had promised.

But he still had the derringer, and the next time maybe he would get to use it.

Chapter 6

The next morning, as Longarm and the others tramped across the yard to the cookshack for breakfast, they saw Chin's body hanging from a meat hook tied to the branch of a tree just outside the cookshack.

To Longarm, his frail body seemed to have shrunk as it hung in the gray light, the old man's queue cut off and stuffed in his mouth—a terrible insult to a Chinaman. Chin's fellow countrymen wilted visibly as they passed this macabre reminder of their helplessness at the hands of Pincherman and his henchmen.

Charlie Fiddle shook his head. "This ought to discourage any more of 'em from throwin' in with that bastard Pincherman."

"Maybe so . . . but it means we've got to keep our heads down for a while. Pincherman will be watching us pretty close."

"Damn," said Burt. "And I was hopin' to shake this place."

"You will, you will," said Longarm.

He ducked his head as he entered the cookshack, wishing he felt as confident as he sounded.

A week later Longarm was leaving the mine shaft when he caught sight of a surrey entering the canyon. The surrey's driver was Hartridge and sitting beside him was Lotus, dressed handsomely in a high-necked pea-green riding outfit. The two horses that pulled the surrey were frisky, high-stepping blacks, and though the sun was close to setting, Hartridge and Lotus gave Longarm the impression of a happy couple out for a Sunday drive.

Longarm kept going, heading for the cookshack, his stomach rumbling even for the filthy grub he knew was waiting. About twenty yards from the cookshack, he had to pull up suddenly as Hartridge stopped the surrey directly in front of him.

"Well, now," said Hartridge, grinning down at Longarm. "Don't tell me you're still with us, Marshal. I thought you'd either be dead or long gone from here."

As Longarm looked up at Hartridge, he kept his eyes averted from Lotus. "That's right. So maybe you better figure out pretty quick what to do with me."

Hartridge chuckled. "Hell, Marshal, we already got that figured. Right now we got you right where we want you. Yes, sir, it ain't often we get to have a real deputy U. S. marshal working this hard for us. And we both kind of like it."

With a mean chuckle, Hartridge slapped the reins and the surrey moved on toward Pincherman's living quarters. Longarm stood for a moment watching them go, then continued on to the cookshack.

Later that evening, Longarm found himself by the window, trying to figure out what part Lotus was playing in all this, especially what her relationship was to Hartridge.

He found it difficult to believe she could find any comfort in that pig's bed. But did that consideration make any difference with a woman? He had known some who would be capable of sleeping with the devil himself if that was what it took to get what they wanted.

Longarm heard Charlie Fiddle moving up beside him. "Did you know that Chinese woman Hartridge brought up here?"

"Sure. I know her. She owns a hotel in Green's Creek."

"You stay at the hotel?"

"That's right. Where else?"

Charlie chuckled. "Nice gal, ain't she?"

"You might say that."

"I know her, too," said Burt, joining them at the window. "She's Hartridge's bird dog. Helps him round up all the stray orientals left in these hills. The way I understand it, as soon as one of these coolies wanders into Green's Creek, she takes him in—all sweetness and consideration, mind you—and the next thing you know, he's been packed off to this place or some other mine."

Longarm took a deep breath. It was hard to believe, but it made sense, assuming Burt was telling the truth. "I was wondering," Longarm admitted, "where Hartridge got all these coolies."

"It's a rotten shame," Charlie Fiddle said. "You'd think she'd have a bad conscience, selling her own people into slavery like that."

"Hell," said Burt, "that don't bother them none. They ain't even Christian."

Longarm looked at Burt. "You mean you can see any difference between a Christian and an oriental in this place?"

"Well, hell, Longarm—you know what I mean."

"No, I sure as hell don't. That's the trouble."

Longarm turned away from the window and, shuffling his chains carefully, moved back to his cot. With patient care, he lifted his feet off the floor, coiled the chains onto the foot of his cot, then dropped his feet down onto them. Then he crossed his arms under his head and stared up at the ceiling, thinking of Lotus Wong.

Longarm was not aware of having fallen asleep until he felt Burt's hand on his shoulder, shaking him awake. He sat up quickly.

"What is it?" he asked Burt.

"Over there. Under the door. See it?"

Longarm glanced over and saw what appeared to be a letter on the floor just inside the door. It had not been there when they went to bed. Someone had taken the risk of stuffing it under the doorway.

Longarm swung his feet carefully down onto the floor so that the chains did not cause any undue disturbance, then moved as quickly as possible over to the envelope. Picking it up, he went over to the window and opened it. By that time Charlie Fiddle and Sanchez had joined them. As Longarm tore open the envelope, a key fell to the floor.

"Jesus!" said Burt, snatching it up. "This looks like the key to our manacles."

"What's the note say?" asked Charlie Fiddle.

Longarm held the letter up to the moonlight. The handwriting was exquisite, small, and as easy to read as print. He read the message aloud softly to the others.

Longarm,

This key will unlock your chains. I have bribed the two guards outside your door. They will not stop you.

I will be waiting in the stable with saddled horses. Wait until after midnight.

Lotus

Burt had already unshackled himself while he listened. He gave the key to Longarm, who put down the letter and unlocked the collars around his ankles, then handed the key to Sanchez. Then he glanced up at the night sky. He had no way to tell the time for sure, but it looked to him from the placement of the Big Dipper that it was pretty close to midnight. Still, he could not be absolutely sure. Best to wait and make sure they did not leave too soon.

Sanchez gave the key to Charlie and moved up beside Longarm. "*Amigo,* this here Lotus woman—you think she can be trusted?"

Longarm shrugged. "How can a man tell such a thing?"

"*Bueno,*" Sanchez replied, his white teeth flashing in his swarthy face. "It is good you understand this. Another thing, *amigo*. What about us?"

"Us?"

"Burt and me—an' old Charlie—we will be coming with you, no? We will need horses, too."

"Don't worry about that now."

"That's right," Charlie said, stopping beside them and dropping his chains onto his cot. "We got to worry about getting out of here first. This could be another trick of Pincherman's."

"You think he's behind that letter?" Burt asked.

Charlie snorted. "I wouldn't put nothin' past that bastard. He ain't human, that animal."

"If you're free now," Longarm told Charlie, "take the key over to the coolies and get them started."

"You mean they's goin' out with us?"

"Not until after we go—and make sure you tell them that."

As Charlie hurried over to the huddled, now wide-awake orientals, Longarm walked over to the spot where he had hidden his watch and derringer, pulled up the board, and retrieved them. Unsnapping the small pistol from its chain, he stuffed the watch into his only remaining pants pocket and shoved the gun into his belt.

Longarm slumped down on his cot and glanced over at Sanchez. The Mexican had been standing by the door, his ear to it, listening. He caught Longarm's glance and walked over to him.

"I think the guards are gone," he told Longarm. "I don't hear nothin' out there. But still I don' like it."

"What choice we got?" Burt asked. "This is our best chance. We got no chains to slow us now."

"Maybe so," Sanchez admitted. "But I think maybe we should not go out through the front door."

Longarm glanced at him. "How then?"

Sanchez left the cot and beckoned to Longarm, who followed Sanchez to the back corner of the building. Positioning himself carefully, Sanchez braced himself, then lowered his shoulder and leaned against the two corner boards. Grimacing at his exertion, he pushed. Slowly the two boards bulged out. Sanchez increased his exertion. Creaking loudly, the boards seemed in danger of snapping. Then came the sound of nails squealing, and a moment later the bottom of both boards pulled free of the sill and swung out suddenly.

Sanchez almost catapulted himself out through the opening. Catching himself in time, he beckoned to Longarm to come closer and look down. Longarm did so and saw one of the beams on which the building was resting and, less then ten feet below them, the slanting ground.

"I say we drop to the ground here," said Sanchez, "keep

low, and circle around to the stable. If it is a trap, Pincherman will be expecting us to make the break out the front door in plain sight."

Longarm nodded quickly. "Done."

Charlie Fiddle moved up beside them and peered down. "How come you didn't show us this little trick before, Sanchez?"

Sanchez grinned. "I think maybe I wait for right opportunity. Now I think is right time. We will have horses waiting and no guards on the porch." He nudged Longarm. "And don't forget, now we have Longarm's big gun. With such a weapon, we will blow them all away!"

Burt pulled up beside them. "The chinks are all loose now. I told them. They won't try to get out until we're free of the place."

"Tell them to leave this way," Longarm said, pointing to the hole in the floor. "Tell them it will be safer."

Burt hurried back to the coolies.

Longarm walked over to the window and peered up at the night sky until he found the Dipper again. This time there was no doubt of it. It was close to midnight. Checking to make sure his derringer was tucked solidly into his belt, he stepped away from the window and walked back to the hole. He lowered himself down through it, hung for a moment on the edge of the floor, then dropped to the ground. The surface was covered with loose shale and the ground sloped so sharply he was forced to grab the piling to keep himself from rolling down the incline.

Stepping out of the way, he waved to the others to follow after him. Sanchez came next, then Charlie Fiddle. Charlie experienced some difficulty getting through the hole, and both Longarm and Sanchez caught him before he hit the ground. As Longarm scrambled up the slope and under the porch, Burt dropped through behind them.

A quick inspection proved that Sanchez was right. There

was no one on the porch above him. But, as Longarm peered across the compound, he thought he glimpsed two shadowy figures crouched behind one of the ore wagons. He beckoned to Sanchez.

"Can you see anyone behind that second wagon?" Longarm asked.

Sanchez peered at it for a long moment. "I cannot tell. There is not enough light."

Longarm looked over at the livery stable. It appeared empty enough, its big doors swung wide.

"We'll go around," Longarm told Sanchez. "It'll take longer, but it's safer."

Sanchez nodded and the two returned to the others. After a brief discussion, it was agreed that Longarm should lead the way, since he was the only one with a weapon—laughable though it might be. Following a gully, they came out eventually near the mine shaft behind the loading chutes. The waiting ore wagons offered excellent cover as they scrambled silently out of the gully and darted the hundred or so yards to the stable. Longarm was the first to reach the barn, with Burt and the others right behind him.

"Look!" cried Burt, pointing back to their sleeping quarters.

They all glanced back. The night seemed alive with swift-moving shadows as the orientals swarmed down through the hole Sanchez had provided.

At that moment a cry came from one of the ore wagons and a shot lanced the night. A coolie appeared to fall, but the rest kept coming. Immediately, there were other shots and Longarm heard Pincherman's overseers as they called out the alarm in a desperate, futile attempt to hold back the swarm of coolies now filling the night. Longarm saw one of the coolies swinging his chain as he mixed it up with one of Pincherman's guards. The guard went down. Snatching up his rifle, the coolie swept on.

Crouching just inside the barn doorway, the three men watched.

"They're headin' for the cookshack," Charlie said.

Longarm nodded. "They've got the key. Soon every oriental in this place will be free. This is what I counted on. A diversion. Now we got it, let's go!"

Turning about, the men darted farther into the barn just as Lotus stepped hurriedly into view from its rear.

"Hurry, Longarm!" she called urgently, as she ran toward him. He saw that her face was streaming with perspiration, as if she had been running very hard to reach the stable in time.

When she saw the three men with him, she pulled up in some confusion. "But I have only saddled two horses!" she exclaimed. "I did not know these others would be with you!"

"They can find horses of their own. It doesn't matter."

As the three men hurriedly saddled mounts for themselves, Longarm and Lotus mounted the two blacks she had already saddled. They were the same high-stepping blacks that had pulled Lotus's surrey earlier that same day. The tumult outside the barn was increasing in volume. There were screams at times, mingled with the shots—and Longarm realized how effective those chains the coolies were wielding could be on a dark night such as this one.

Charlie, Burt, and Sanchez finished saddling the horses and swung up into the saddles.

"We're ready," Burt told Longarm.

Longarm glanced at Lotus. "We'll follow you," he told her. "Which way are we going?"

She pointed to the rear of the barn. "Toward the hills. There's a canyon. If we follow it, it will take us out of this valley."

"Let's go, then," Longarm told her.

As they clattered out through the barn's rear door, then struck off toward the lowering hills, Longarm heard the hoist engines in the main shaft building behind him suddenly cut out. The sudden silence was as noticeable as a thunderclap on a cloudless day. Glancing back, they saw flames lighting the sky as the shaft buildings went up. Meanwhile, the rattle of gunfire and the faint screams of assaulted men rose to a crescendo.

The coolies were settling old scores.

Not long after, as the five riders entered the mouth of the canyon Lotus had mentioned, Longarm pulled up.

Swinging her horse around to face him, Lotus cried, "Why are you stopping here?"

"What is it?" asked Sanchez, pulling up also.

"The rest of you follow Lotus," Longarm told them. "I'll catch up. It won't be hard for me to follow this canyon."

"But where in blazes are you going, *amigo?*"

Back."

"Going back?" Charlie cried. "You crazy or something? What in hell for? We just got out of there!"

"I'm going after Running Moon. I can't leave her to those butchers."

Lotus had ridden back to him. "So you go back for the Indian? The one they capture with you?"

"Yes."

"Do you know where she is?"

"On the second floor. Over the saloon."

"Then I must warn you," Lotus said. "She is not with the other girls. This night that pig Pincherman and that odious toad who follows him about have taken her to a cabin on the flat. It is among some cottonwoods, far from the mine. They wanted privacy."

Longarm nodded. "Thanks, Lotus."

"You want me to go back with you?" asked Sanchez.

"No. Keep going with Lotus. All of you. I told you, I'll catch up."

"You are a fool," said Lotus. "We will wait for you in canyon."

Longarm swung his horse about and galloped back toward the mine.

When he arrived back, there were fires everywhere and sporadic shooting, with men running this way and that through the darkness. Longarm caught glimpses of coolies hiding fearfully among the rocks, and others scurrying for the hills. He dismounted in the darkness and led his horse behind the saloon. He spotted the cottonwoods in the distance.

He mounted up and, keeping to the shadows, crossed the flat, tethered the black in the cottonwoods, and headed for the cabin. It was deep in the timber on the far side, the timber screening the canyon and mine completely. Just as he reached one corner of the cabin, the door to the cabin swung open. Light flooded across the steps and out into the yard. Jody appeared in the doorway and emptied a slops jar. He was about to close the door when he paused.

"Hey, you fellows!" he called. "Come here!"

Longarm flattened himself against the wall.

As soon as Jody was joined by his companions in the doorway, he held up a finger and said, "Listen! You hear that?"

"What do you mean?" said someone behind him. "I don't hear nothing."

"That's what I mean! The engines've stopped."

"So they stopped," another one said. "So what? Let Hartridge handle it. We got other business."

This comment brought a sudden bark of laughter, and the door was pushed shut.

Longarm waited a moment, then moved along the side of the cabin until he came to a side window. Peering in, he saw Jody and three others sitting around a poker table, bottles on the floor beside them. He did not see Pincherman.

Moving with the silence of a shadow, Longarm made his way to the rear of the cabin, past the privy, and came to a couple of windows. Their panes were thick with dust and grime. Wiping off the dirt carefully, he found himself looking into the bedroom.

He had found Running Moon. She was lying down on a huge brass bed, naked, with only a torn, motheaten blanket thrown over her slim body. Her head was turned away so that he could not see her face. She was spread-eagled, her wrists tied to opposite bedposts at the head of the bed, her ankles to the foot.

Stepping into view from close beside the window, Pincherman reached over and shook Running Moon violently. There was no response. Kneeling on the bed, he took her shoulders and flung her over so that she was looking up at him. Longarm winced. Running Moon's face looked as if a hammer had been used on it. It was swollen grotesquely. One eye was completely closed, her nose was a bloody mess, her mouth torn cruelly.

And she was not responding.

Pincherman stood up and bellowed to someone he called Blackie. A chunky fellow with black hair and blacker eyes stepped into the bedroom. His back to the wall, his ear close to the window's edge, Longarm caught most of the conversation.

"What in hell did you do to her?" Pincherman demanded.

"I knocked some sense into her," the other one replied, his voice harsh and surly. "She just laid there. I couldn't get no response."

"What'd you use on her?"

There was a short bark of laughter. "Just my fists."

"Well, she's out now, and I can't bring her around."

"Hell, I'll fix that."

Longarm heard his heavy tread fade as Blackie went

back into the other room. He returned a moment later, walked over to the bed, and hurled a cup of whiskey in Running Moon's face. It didn't do much good, so he poured more whiskey into the cup and threw that at her as well.

Still there was no response.

"No sense in wasting good whiskey," Blackie said with a shrug. He turned and walked out of the room.

Pincherman hesitated a moment, glanced once more at Running Moon, then followed Blackie out with a resigned shrug, slamming the door behind him.

At once Longarm reached up and tried to lift the window sash, but it held fast. Dirt had encrusted its edges and now held the frame solidly. He tried again, heaving up desperately, and this time the sash gave just a little. It was not much, but it proved that the sash could be moved. He heaved one more time. Blood pounded in his temples as he slowly, steadily lifted the sash high enough for him to be able to boost himself over the windowsill and into the room.

Moving swiftly to the bedroom door, Longarm opened it a crack and peered into the other room. Pincherman was sitting at the table with his back to Longarm. Blackie was sitting across from him. Jody was on Pincherman's right, and a fourth man, whom Longarm recognized as one of the winch engineers, sat at Pincherman's left.

The room was a shambles. Cots and tables were strewn haphazardly about; empty bottles and overturned jugs lay everywhere. All four men were puffing on cigars, and the air above their heads was blue with swirling coils of smoke. They had taken off their vests and their gunbelts were draped over the backs of their chairs. So intent were the four men on their drinking and their poker that they never once glanced in Longarm's direction.

Longarm closed the door again and hurried over to Running Moon's side. He leaned close and called to her softly. When she didn't respond, he untied her wrists and ankles, working with feverish haste. After he had freed her, he bent again to awaken her, his lips close to hers as he whispered her name.

He shrank back, dismayed. He could detect no breath. Dropping his hand to her brow, he found it was ice cold.

He stepped away from the bed and for a long moment looked down at the dead girl. Then he turned and stared at the door. He could hear the men in the other room still playing poker. Occasional bursts of laughter broke through the steady murmur of their rough voices. They had no inkling of what they had done.

There was only one filthy sheet on the bed. Pulling it out from under her, he covered Running Moon's pathetic nakedness. Then he pulled his derringer from his belt, strode to the bedroom doorway, and pulled it open.

It was Blackie, looking up from his hand, who saw Longarm first. The cigar dropped from his mouth. Jody and the engineer turned to look at him, then hastily scraped back their chairs. Pincherman knocked his chair back and spun to face Longarm. As Jody reached back for his holster, Longarm fired. The round caught him in the chest, punching him back away from the table. He crashed heavily to the floor.

Pincherman was reaching down for his holster under his overturned chair when Longarm kicked him in the head hard enough to send him looping into the engineer. By this time Blackie had drawn his sixgun and was lifting it to fire when Longarm swept the kerosene lamp off the table and hurled it at him.

The lamp caught Blackie square in the chest. A bright blossom of fire exploded on his shirt front, then leaped upward, engulfing his neck and mouth. Blackie dropped his gun and, screaming, began clawing at his face.

Tucking the derringer into his belt, Longarm snatched

up Pincherman's Colt and leveled it on Pincherman and the engineer.

"Don't!" shrieked Pincherman. "Please! Don't shoot! You're a lawman. It would be murder!"

Longarm smiled thinly. "All right, then. I won't shoot."

Snatching up another lamp, he flung it at their feet. The floor exploded into flames. As the flames crackled hungrily across the floor, the two men shrank back, terrified, then turned and bolted for the door. A third lamp was sitting on a bureau behind Longarm. He flung it at the wall close by the door. At once flames covered it and the walls around it, then began licking hungrily at the low ceiling. The two men ducked their heads and cowered back, glancing in terror at Longarm. Black, choking clouds now filled the room.

Slowly, still covering Pincherman and the engineer, Longarm backed up, waiting for the terrified men to rush him, hoping they would, since he was now blocking them from the only route to safety that remained—the bedroom and the window leading from it.

"Come on, you bastards," Longarm taunted. "Which one of you is going to be first?"

Pincherman was. He put his head down and charged Longarm. As he materialized out of the wall of flame now engulfing the poker table and floor, Longarm fired low, catching Pincherman in the knees. With a scream, Pincherman collapsed back into the flames, his face shriveling, his hair transformed instantly into a bright torch.

Next came the engineer.

Longarm waited for this one to clear the flames completely before sending two quick slugs into his heart. The man staggered, smashed into the wall beside Longarm, then slipped to the ground. Reaching down, Longarm caught him by the nape of the neck and dragged him into the bedroom. Kicking the door shut, he flung him down at the foot of

Running Moon's bed. He strapped on the engineer's gunbelt and dropped Pincherman's Colt into the holster. Then he opened the bedroom door a crack and peered into the other room.

It was a thundering mass of flames by this time, the heat so searing that Longarm felt his eyebrows begin to curl. He stepped back and pulled open the bedroom door. Great tongues of flame roared into the bedroom, as if they were exploding from the mouth of a furnace.

Longarm hurried to the window and lowered himself to the ground. As he trotted through the cottonwoods to his horse, he glanced back and saw the cabin completely engulfed in flames—Running Moon's funeral pyre, and with that dog at her feet, Longarm had seen to it that she had a Viking's funeral.

Mounting up, he spurred his horse back the way he had come.

Chapter 7

Approaching the mine, Longarm still heard sporadic shooting, but it seemed to have calmed down considerably, and the fires were out. The hoist engines remained silent, however, and there seemed to be considerable confusion from those still trying to get things back to normal. Longarm's guess was that a good number—but not all—of the coolies had escaped. If nothing else, the mine Hartridge was responsible for keeping running was going to have an immediate and perhaps prolonged shutdown.

Slipping behind the shaft buildings, he dismounted and led his horse after him through the darkness, keeping as close as possible to the slope. It would have been better if he could have muffled the horse's hoofs, but he had no time for that. Rounding a huge pile of slag, he found himself facing a nervous engineer, one Longarm vaguely recognized.

"Stay where you are, you son of a bitch!" the man cried, his voice revealing that he was close to hysteria. "Don't take another step. And unbuckle your gunbelt."

Longarm hesitated.

"Do it!"

Slowly and carefully, Longarm unbuckled his gunbelt and let it drop, his right hand closing about the derringer he had stuck in his belt, the darkness effectively concealing his action. The enormous Colt the engineer was holding wavered uncertainly. Longarm saw that the engineer's right shoulder was gleaming darkly. He had been shot. In addition, it appeared that his clothes had been nearly torn from his back. There was excellent reason for his panic.

"Why not put down that gun?" Longarm suggested quietly. "Hell, I'm not going to hurt you. I just want to ride out of here and put this place behind me."

"I can't let you do that!" the engineer cried, cocking his weapon and taking a sudden step back. He licked his lips frantically. "You're a damned convict! I'm going to have to kill you!"

The engineer was in no condition to think clearly. He was not truly responsible for his actions. Longarm sympathized with him. But that big Colt in his hand could kill just as surely as if he *were* responsible.

Throwing himself to one side, Longarm flung up his derringer and fired at the man. The engineer was hit low, in the thigh, and the force of the bullet sent him stumbling backward. As he did so, his Colt went off, the shot going wild. Longarm leaped to his feet and rushed the man. They grappled clumsily for a moment, then Longarm twisted the Colt out of the engineer's hand and clubbed the fellow to the ground. When he tried to get up, Longarm again brought the barrel down on his head, this time knocking him senseless.

Longarm knew he had hit the man, but there was no blood. He examined the man swiftly and found in his side pocket a leather pouch filled with gold coins. There was a hole in the pocket and the pouch where the slug had pounded through. The coins, bent slightly, had absorbed most of the bullet's impact, leaving only a bruise on the engineer's thigh.

Pocketing the gold, Longarm picked up his derringer and the gunbelt and remounted. Ahead of him he could see dimly the mouth of the canyon where he had left Lotus and the others. He was anxious to reach it before the sound of this brief gun battle drew any of Hartridge's men to investigate.

As soon as he reached the canyon and felt its welcome darkness close about him, he lifted his mount to a lope and put the mine and all the horror it represented behind him.

A little after dawn, he was nearing the end of the canyon when he heard a faint shout from high above him. Glancing up, he saw Charlie Fiddle waving a hat. As soon as he had caught Longarm's attention, Charlie pointed to a trail off to Longarm's right. Longarm turned his mount toward it and before long the game trail had lifted him to the canyon's rim. Charlie and the rest had dismounted and were waiting for him. Behind them, the remains of a campfire was still smoldering.

It was Lotus who spoke first, as Longarm pulled up alongside them and dismounted. "Where's the Indian girl?"

"Dead."

She frowned. "Did you find her with Pincherman, as I told you?"

"I did."

"What of Pincherman and the others?"

"Dead."

Her eyebrows lifted. "You are some lawman, Custis," she said, her voice close to disappointment. "You do not die easily."

Charlie Fiddle broke into the discussion by handing Longarm a cup of coffee. Longarm thanked the old man and sipped the coffee gratefully.

"What about the mine?" asked Burt.

"They got the fires under control, but the engines still weren't working when I left. I figure quite a few of the coolies got away."

"Enough to shut down the mine?" asked Lotus.

"For a while, anyway."

"I must get back to Green's Creek," Lotus told him. "I am glad you are no longer in Hartridge's hands, Custis."

Longarm finished his coffee, threw the dregs on the ashes, then handed the cup back to Charlie. Turning to Lotus, he took her by the arm and steered her away from the others. "That fellow you sent after me. Abe Goshen. I think you should know. He's dead."

She frowned. "Did you . . . ?"

"No. It was a stray bullet from Tomlinson's gun killed him."

"When he didn't return, I was afraid something might have happened to him. His sister works for me. It will be a terrible blow to her. And I'm sorry, myself. He was a good man."

"Why did you send him after me?"

"I learned that Sharlow's cabin had been burnt down. In that case, I was almost certain Sharlow and Tomlinson would be holed up in Maria. I sent him to warn you—to help you if he could."

Longarm wanted to believe her, but he couldn't. "Well, he wasn't much help, I'm afraid. Thanks anyway."

"Are you still going after Tomlinson?"

"It's Hartridge I want. After what happened to Black

Feather and Running Moon, I want him bad. Tomlinson can wait for now. If Hartridge is your friend, I suggest you pray for him."

She smiled coldly. "No man is my friend, Custis. I use them just as they use me."

Longarm almost shivered at the cold heartlessness of that remark; and looking into her eyes, he realized she meant it—every word. "In that case, why all the concern about me—this breakout, for instance."

She shrugged. "I told you."

"You want a chance to outlast me."

"Yes."

"Why?"

"It is against nature for a man—any man—to outlast a woman, especially this woman."

Again she was refusing to tell Longarm what she was after, what her real game was. But he knew that when it served her purpose to tell him, she would.

A moment later, standing with Charlie Fiddle and the others, he waved goodbye to her as she rode off. The look in her eye as she glanced down at him for a moment had sent a cold chill down his back.

He was not Lotus's enemy now—not that he knew of, at any rate—and he hoped he never became one.

An hour or so later, they picked up a wide trail worn pretty bare with wagon tracks. Anxious to get to a town where he could get cleaned up and telegraph Vail, Longarm decided to follow the tracks. There was no protest from the others, and they set off.

By midday their way was blocked by a formidable mountain barrier, the roadway heading for a high pass at a steep grade. It promised to be quite a climb. Longarm pulled up and contemplated the trail ahead, wondering if it was a good idea to follow this trail any farther. Charlie Fiddle stopped beside him and wound his reins about his saddlehorn. He appeared to be thinking the same thing as Longarm as he contemplated the formidable barrier that lay across their path.

"You know this country?" Longarm asked him.

"I ain't never been this way before, and that's the truth. This country's got as many valleys and canyons as a jigsaw has pieces. But the way I look at it, wagon tracks have to lead somewhere—and usually do."

Longarm glanced at Burt and Sanchez. Both men shrugged.

"We'll go on then," said Longarm.

By the time they reached the pass, it was mid-afternoon and they were well past the timberline. They found themselves looking down at the tops of pines almost a quarter of a mile below them. On their way through the pass, the men had dismounted to give their horses a break, mounting up again only when, still following the wagon tracks, they had regained the timber.

Riding beside him, Burt glanced at Longarm, a wry smile on his face. "I was thinkin'. If there *is* a town up here, it's probably run by mountain goats."

Longarm chuckled.

Sanchez and Charlie Fiddle pulled alongside. It was clear they had something on their minds and had come to some sort of conclusion. Sanchez cleared his throat first. Longarm glanced at him.

"What's on your mind, Sanchez?"

"Me and Charlie, we wondered what you're up to. We mean, beside getting some clothes and telegraphin' your boss."

"Up to?"

"Yeah. You goin' after that red-headed feller you told us about, or you goin' after Hartridge?"

"Hartridge."

"I thought you was a lawman," piped up Charlie Fiddle.

"I am."

"Well, you ain't got no warrant for Hartridge, have you?"

"That don't matter. I want him."

Sanchez grinned. "So maybe you ain't all lawman, eh, *amigo?"*

Longarm peered carefully at Sanchez. "You wouldn't be worried about yourself now, would you, Sanchez?"

"Not if you tell me I don't have to worry."

"You don't have to worry."

Sanchez's smile lighted his dark, handsome face brilliantly. "That's good enough for me, *amigo.*"

"The thing is," said Charlie Fiddle, "we'd both of us like to go after that bastard Hartridge."

"Me, too," said Burt.

"Then consider yourselves my deputies," Longarm told them. "I'll figure out how to make it all legal later."

The three men grinned, obviously relieved. They had suffered longer than Longarm had from Hartridge's heavy hand and were as eager as Longarm to make the son of a bitch pay.

"Say, Longarm," Burt asked, "we've been wonderin'."

"About what?"

"That true what you told the Dragon Lady? Pincherman's dead?"

"He's dead, all right."

"And you killed him?"

Longarm nodded.

"What about Jody?"

"Him, too."

There was an almost audible sigh from his companions. Longarm offered no more details and the three asked for none.

• • •

Close to sundown, the road ahead of them opened up considerably, thc trees falling away also, as they moved on to a high, broad valley. Just ahead of them they saw an extensive marshland, its gleaming surface dotted with islands of willows and beech, the road they were following continuing on across it to a flat on the far side.

They all pulled up to study the flat, Burt standing up in his stirrups to get a better look. What looked like a mining camp occupied the flat. They could see clearly the dim shapes of houses nestled in the lee of a sharply rising mountain flank.

"What the hell is that place, I wonder?" said Burt.

"Bent Rock, maybe," suggested Longarm, "or maybe Bowie."

"We're too high for that to be Bowie," Charlie Fiddle snorted. "And I don't see any railroad tracks or telegraph lines. You won't find this town on any map you can find."

Longarm nodded. Charlie was right. But that didn't mean this place couldn't offer them food and a place to sleep.

"We won't find out nothin' here," Longarm told them. "We'll just have to check it out. Let's go. I'm hungry."

"All's I want is a bottle," said Charlie Fiddle, smacking his lips, "and some fresh chewin' tobaccy."

"Sheets is what I want," said Sanchez. "Clean sheets on a bed, and no chains on my feet when I wake up."

"There's somethin' else *I* want," said Burt, grinning.

No one needed to ask him what that was. They lifted their mounts to a canter and headed for the marshland and the town on the distant flat beyond.

The ride across the marshland took longer than they had expected, so circuitous was the road. At places it was only wide enough for the wagon tracks they were still following. In more than a few places, Longarm could see where the roadway had been widened with pilings and in some cases boulders to accommodate the wagons, an indication that the road across this marsh had not been there until the town's builders put it there.

It was near dusk when they found they had to cross a bridge before reaching the flat—a curious bridge that aroused their curiosity the moment they saw it.

The bridge was unusual both in structure and in design. It arched high over the waterway it spanned, and set apart from the bridge's main roadway was a pedestrian walkway. The bridge itself was supported by a complicated network of cantilevered struts. In addition, the planking that made up the floor was lengthwise, not crosswise, and was made up of solid beams.

The most intriguing feature was the carved heads of lions set up on pedestals on both ends of the bridge. As the men rode closer, it became clear how delicately carved was the fretwork that covered the beams holdings up the bridge and the walkway. When at last they clopped over the bridge, its floor gave off a solid, booming sound. This was definitely like no bridge any of them had ever expected to find in such a wild and isolated land. And what Longarm immediately asked himself was what manner of gold or silver miners would spend this much effort and time on a simple bridge.

As they neared the town, Longarm saw how narrow the streets were and how strange-looking were many of the houses that had been built away from the town's main street. A few of them had roofs that extended well out over the sides and then curled up like hatbrims. Perched on a hill high above the town sat a small, strange-looking building with tiny windows and a hatlike roof. In the rays of the setting sun it fairly glowed.

"That's sure a crazy-lookin' buildin' up there," said Charlie, pulling his mount to a halt and pointing to it.

The rest pulled their mounts to a halt also. As Longarm

studied it, a dim memory stirred to life within him. He was almost positive he had seen a building very similar to that somewhere before, but he couldn't quite remember where. And then it came to him. He had seen a drawing of such a building in a *Harper's Weekly* article on the Chinese who had come to America from the Pearl River delta in Canton to help build the railroad, and who had then stayed on to work in the West's mines.

"What you're looking at, gents," Longarm told them, "is a Chinese temple. And that bridge we just crossed over is a prime example of Chinese architecture, if I'm not mistaken."

"Jesus," said Burt softly, his eyes gleaming excitedly. "You sure of that?"

"As sure as I can be."

"What do you think of that, Charlie?" Burt asked.

"I'm way ahead of you!" Charlie said, his voice hushed, his eyes gleaming as he looked up at the Chinese temple. "This must be it! The place where all them slants found the gold!"

Too excited to talk, all Burt could do was nod.

Frowning, Sanchez spurred his mount up beside Longarm. "You believe these two hombres? They've gone plumb loco."

"Maybe we better forget about gold," Charlie drawled, "and get ready to meet those gents up ahead of us. They look a mite upset."

"I been noticin'," said Longarm.

Though it was getting dark rapidly now and the town was still some distance away, the four men could see at once that all of the men in the crowd gathering before them were Chinese, dressed in their traditional garb, dark trousers and tunics. A few were wearing their odd conical headgear as well, and most of them seemed to be carrying weapons of one sort or another.

"Yup," said Charlie happily, "they're all slants! Every mother's son of them!" He glanced at Sanchez. "You see? What'd I tell you?"

"Whoever they are," muttered Sanchez, "they sure don' look friendly."

"Keep going," said Longarm. "It's getting dark and I'm still hungry."

The four men, riding abreast, urged their mounts forward and kept to a leisurely walk until they got to within a hundred yards of the glowering crowd of orientals. Then they pulled up.

"What now?" Burt asked Longarm nervously.

"Wait."

After a moment or two, one of the Chinese stepped cautiously out of the crowd and began to walk toward them. He was a very old man, his face lean and incredibly wrinkled with a light, cottony tuft of feathery whiskers on his chin. He had on a small, black cap that covered only the top of his head, and he kept his hands clasped together inside his wide sleeves. When he came to within ten yards of them, he stopped and bowed politely.

"I am Ling Chan," he told them in excellent English, his voice thin but strong. "I am but a faceless stone that lies upon the side of the road. These men at my back are only insignificant wretches, worthless chaff the wind has not yet decided to blow away. Why, then, Most Honorable Knights of the Road, do you bother to journey to such a miserable town as this?"

"That was real pretty," replied Longarm. "And I sure do wish I could reply just as pretty. But I can't, Mr. Chan. What's the name of this place?"

Ling Chan bowed. "Celestial City," he replied, with just the hint of mockery in his tone.

"Well, all me and my three worn-out knights are hoping for is a place to stay, a chance to freshen up, and maybe to eat some of your fine Chinese cooking." Longarm smiled blandly. "Then we'll be on our way."

"And this is all the honorable knights wish?"

"That's it. I was hoping for a telegraph or an express office too, but it looks to me like that wouldn't be available."

"Alas, no, my friend," said Ling Chan. "This unworthy place has no such wondrous inventions. You are quite correct."

Longarm smiled. "Then we are welcome to stay the night?"

Ling Chan bowed. "Of course. And, for that courtesy, there is only one small concession we require."

"And what's that?"

"Your weapons. Please to take them off while you are in our miserable little metropolis."

"It's a deal."

Turning around, Ling Chan shouted something in Chinese to the group blocking the road. They dispersed at once, the men melting back into the stores and buildings that lined the main street. Turning back to Longarm, Ling Chan pointed to a large two-story building further down the street.

"There is the hotel," he said. "And you will find a livery stable across the street from it."

"Much obliged," Longarm said.

The old Chinese gentleman bowed, turned, and moved off down the center of the street, as if he had designated himself as their guide. Longarm unwound his reins from the saddlehorn and nudged his horse after him.

Keeping up beside him, Burt muttered, "At least the old bastard didn't call the hotel miserable."

"Nor the livery stable," agreed Charlie Fiddle.

"Maybe that's a good sign."

As they rode farther on into the town, they found lining both sides of the main street the usual complement of clapboard buildings containing harness shops, barbershops, saloons, general stores, and a feed mill at the far end of town. To all outward appearances, the town was pretty much what a man would expect in any Western cowtown.

But this was sure as hell not a typical cowtown. And more than likely, Longarm mused, it had a few surprises in store for them.

Chapter 8

Later that same evening, while the others took their turns bathing in the back of the barbershop, Longarm found a tailor still open for business.

Earlier Longarm had bathed in a tall pine barrel into which buckets of steaming hot water had been poured, the result being a near-scalding bath that had peeled off the layers of grime and drained his pores completely, cleansing him finally of his own awesome, unwashed stench. A man was not supposed to be able to know how bad he smelled, but Longarm could testify that such a claim was nonsense, as he knew from bitter experience. What he wanted now was clean, new clothes—and the sooner the better.

As he opened the door to the tailor shop, a bell on the door tinkled, alerting the tailor. At once a small, stoop-shouldered little Chinaman stepped through a curtained doorway behind the counter. He had an elfin, puckered face, soft white hair, and a long gray queue that extended down almost to his waist. He clasped his hands before him and bowed twice, eagerly.

"I am Chou Li-Fan. Welcome to my humble establishment," he said in such mangled English Longarm was barely able to understand him.

"I'd like a complete outfit—coat, vest, and pants," Longarm told him.

The old tailor nodded quickly. "Yes, yes. I see." He grinned suddenly and plucked at Longarm's filthy, torn frock coat and then at his tattered, filthy trousers. "No good no more," he cackled, laughing. "No good. Too much work."

"And I'd like underclothes and a hat."

"Closs street, maybe," the old man said, pointing. "They have hat in store. You see."

"All right, I'll do that. But will you make the suit?"

The tailor nodded quickly. "I make suit, yes. Velly nice, I make it!"

"Good. How soon?"

"Tomorrow be fine?"

"It sure would," Longarm told him, delighted at such quick service.

The old man plucked at Longarm's torn sleeve and drew him gently through the curtains and into the back room. From another curtained doorway stepped an exquisitely proportioned Chinese girl in her twenties. She was tall and slim, the top of her head coming almost to Longarm's chin.

"This my miserable daughter," the tailor said, in obvious despair. "She is Ti-Ling. Most unworthy daughter. But she help some, maybe."

He turned and vanished back into the front of the shop.

Ti-Ling was snugly attired in a black silk jacket and a long, tight-fitting skirt that reached all the way down to her lavender slippers. A slit in the side of her skirt revealed a generous portion of her dusky thigh.

Bowing slightly, her hands clasped before her, she stepped forward to help Longarm out of his ruined clothing. Longarm took out his gold coins and placed them on a nearby table as Ti-Ling bent to help Longarm pull off his boots. Then she took his frock coat, his vest, and his tattered and bloody shirt, after which, without blushing or pulling away, she helped him peel out of his pants and longjohns.

Stepping back, she took up the tattered remains of his once proud brown tweed frock coat and pants and walked over to a chair in the corner. There was a robe hanging on a hook near the doorway behind her, and he expected her to reach over and hand it to him. But not until she had finished folding his clothes over the back of the chair did she reach back for the robe. Turning with it in her hands, she let her gleaming black eyes sweep over his tall, naked frame. So bold and provocative was this one glance that Longarm felt himself come alive, as if her eyes alone had been sufficient to breathe fire into his loins.

His reaction to her glance was compelling and not a bit inconspicuous. It did not go unnoticed. For an instant, a barely perceptible smile lightened the girl's face as she handed him his robe, a dark red, luxurious garment, silken to the touch. Gliding swiftly behind him, she helped him into it. As she did so, he could feel her breath, like some exotic perfume, on the back of his neck. As she moved back around in front of him, he followed her with his eyes and smiled. Her lips did not smile back, but her eyes—glowing with a sudden, eager warmth—did.

At that moment, her father reappeared with his tape measure. Working swiftly, he sang out the measurements to Ti-Ling in a high singsong dialect that was totally incomprehensible to Longarm, while the girl noted them down swiftly with a pencil stub. When the old man had finished, Ti-Ling handed him the paper with the measurements on it, and he vanished back into a closet behind Longarm. He returned a moment later with bolts of tweed cloth piled high in his arms and indicated with a nod of his head that Longarm was to choose which material he wanted. As Longarm struggled to make his choice, he was astonished at the quality of the cloth in such an isolated town.

"You have money for this?" the Chinaman asked quickly after Longarm had chosen perhaps the finest cloth available—a brown tweed, very close in quality to the material in his ruined suit.

Longarm reached over for the pouch he had taken from his pants and emptied out a few of the gold coins. The old Chinaman's eyes widened as he saw the wealth pouring out.

"What do you think?" Longarm asked.

The tailor nodded quickly. "This be fine!"

Longarm leaned close to the old man and grinned at him. "But don't you try to rob me!"

"No, no! Me no rob! You see! Do velly fine job, yes?"

Laughing, Longarm dropped a couple of coins into the man's hand.

At once the old man took out a pair of scissors and began cutting the cloth from the bolt.

"How long am I going to have to go around in this here robe?" he asked the tailor.

For the first time, the tailor's daughter spoke up, in a clear, musical voice. "What's the matter? Do you not like it?"

Startled, he turned to face her.

"There's nothing wrong with this robe," he told her with a smile, "but it's for inside, not outside, if you know what I mean."

"I understand. Upstairs we have clothes you may wear until my father has finished making your suit." She measured him with her eyes. "But we may have some difficulty finding anything large enough to fit you." She frowned.

"And even if we do, such clothes would not be like what you wear."

Longarm smiled down at her. "Just as long as it keeps the drafts off."

"Surely these clothes will do that," she replied, returning his smile. "Come. Allow me to help you."

Picking up his gold, Longarm followed Ti-Ling deeper into the recesses of the tailor's shop, around a sharp corner, then up a short flight of stairs. At the top of the stairs, she paused in front of a doorway, opened the door for him, and, bowing slightly, allowed him to precede her. When he did, he found himself in an exquisitely furnished bedroom, Ti-Ling's, obviously. At that moment, he realized Ti-Ling had something else in mind besides outfitting him with a temporary wardrobe.

She followed in after him and closed the door firmly. Turning to him, she smiled. "What is your name, please?"

"Long. Custis Long."

She smiled and glanced swiftly down at his crotch. "I am sure the name fits you very well."

"You can call me Custis, if you want. What does Ti-Ling mean?"

"Flower of the night." She smiled. "You see? We are both aptly named. But you may call me Ti."

"You speak English very well."

"My father was a tailor in Denver when I was born. I went to school there before coming here with him."

"Do you miss Denver?"

She frowned. "No. A mob burned my home and killed my mother when she tried to escape. Later, another mob drove my brother and my father from the mines in Leadville. We spent that winter in these mountains. It was not a good winter."

"I am sorry."

"But we do not blame all white men for those few mad

ones. In school I met many westerners who did not care that my skin was yellow or that my eyes are slanted."

"I think you are very beautiful."

"You see? So, it is settled then. We are well suited." She walked boldly toward him and untied the robe's sash. As his robe fell open, she thrust herself hard against his naked crotch. At the same time she put her arms around his neck. They kissed, and as her lips worked his open, he felt himself stir quickly to life, reminding him of just how long it had been.

"You see," she whispered after the kiss, "when I saw how you responded to my glance, I knew at once I had to finish what I started. It would be too unkind to do otherwise—for both of us. I must say, I do miss the tall Denver men. They were very polite. And they knew how to please a woman."

"I'll do my best," he told her, slipping off his robe and letting it fall to the floor.

"I'm sure you will," she responded.

She placed a palm gently against his naked chest and eased him backward until the back of his knees felt the edge of the mattress. Then, with a delighted laugh, as he started to fall backward onto the bed, she flung herself happily upon him. He caught her about the waist and swung her around so that she was lying on the coverlet alongside him.

When she started to take off her blouse and skirt, he stayed her hand. "Let me," he said.

"Of course."

To his delight, when he unbuttoned her jacket he found nothing under it but her golden breasts. He took one large, solid breast in his hands and bent to it, kissing its nipple. Then he kissed her other one, just as gently. She leaned her head back, her fingers in his hair as she pressed his head down more firmly onto her breasts. When she began to moan softly, he slipped her silken skirt from her long legs and ran his hands down her incredibly smooth limbs.

He was on fire now, as was she. Pulling his lips from her breasts, he kissed her on the mouth, his body covering hers, his thighs tightening convulsively around her limbs, drawing all the fire and passion he could from her, hungrily, feverishly, with a brute clumsiness that aroused them both to an even greater pitch. Soon he felt himself being swept along on a tide over which he no longer had any control.

She had managed to release her hair. It cascaded down over his face and neck in wild, intoxicating profusion, a shimmering nightscape of subtle perfume. Meanwhile, she had eased her long body onto his while her lips continued to move hungrily over his face, his neck, his chest. At the same time, her incredible fingers were igniting his crotch, sending a sweet ache up through his loins. Abruptly, she forked a thigh all the way over and mounted him. He was big enough by this time—more than big enough—and she eased herself back onto his shaft with a delighted gasp and with an ease that brought a deep, appreciative sigh from him.

It had been a long time. Too long.

She straightened and he heard her pleased cry as she began to ride him like a pony, a trotting pony, her head thrown back, her marvelously firm, upthrust breasts rocking, her hair an inky cloud coiling about her shoulders and breasts.

Longarm tightened his buttocks and found himself driving up to meet her thrust for thrust as she ground herself down upon his shaft, rotating slowly and crying out softly with each movement. He ran his hands up and down her spine, feeling the tiny bone ridges riding under her silken skin. But he could hold back no longer. He felt a sudden, urgent upsurging from deep within his loins. Grabbing her pelvic bones, he began slamming her recklessly down onto his erection, and came in an explosion that rocked him—

and that seemed to go on forever as he continued to pulse within her.

She could feel him coming inside her, and it drove her wild. With wild abandon, she flung herself down upon his erection until at last, uttering a muffled gasp, she too came. The surge rocked her and he thought she was going to fall off him as she climaxed repeatedly. As she pulsed atop him, she reached out blindly for him. He took hold of her hands and held on as her shuddering pulsations slowly subsided.

After a moment, still gasping with pleasure, she looked down at him and brushed her hair back off her face.

"You are not finished yet, Custis?"

He shook his head.

"Neither am I."

She squeezed his erection tightly with the muscles deep inside her, making it impossible for him to pull out, despite the hot wetness of her. Again she shuddered, grew rigid, and flung her head back, letting out a tiny, delighted cry. It went on for some time, and the warmth now enveloping his vitals sent Longarm rigid once more.

Laughing excitedly, Ti collapsed onto his chest. Her lips sought his and soon they were kissing wildly, her tongue thrusting deep into his mouth. The smell of her was intoxicating, as was the sound of her eager panting, the feel of her perfumed breath on his face. She was all animal now, lust unhitched from any traces, wild, unrestrained.

Aroused now beyond anything he had experienced before, Longarm took charge. He rolled her over and plunged deep inside her. She gasped in surprise and he felt her long fingernails raking down his back. His thrusting became wild, brutal. Beneath him, he saw her shiny breasts jiggling furiously, her tight face a mask of concentration as she stared up at him, her dark eyes fixing his, holding them with a hypnotic gleam that dared him to bring her to orgasm again.

He was part of her now, his flesh riveted to hers. He

moved swiftly up onto the bed for a better purchase and took his time, savoring each thrust, pleased at the sight of her beneath him and the feel of her legs locked firmly around his buttocks. Her eyes suddenly closed as deep, guttural grunts of pleasure broke raggedly from her.

He slowed his thrusts still further then, in order to savor each one and to slow down the inexorable build toward his climax. But this infuriated her. She began to pound futilely on his powerful chest, then raked his back cruelly with her fingernails.

"You bastard!" she hissed. "Come now. I'm coming! I'm coming!"

The look in her eyes did it. He could hold back no longer. With one final, brutal thrust, he came—just as she did. They clung to each other then, panting wildly, allowing the storm to pass. At length, Longarm eased out and rolled off her. She rolled over, clinging to him, so their faces remained close.

Kissing his sweating face and lips, she laughed. "Mmm, you taste so good."

"You're not angry any longer?"

"You are still a bastard, but a nice bastard. You drive a woman crazy, but that is what a woman wants. This one, anyway."

"I am glad you are pleased."

"And what about me? Did I please you?" she asked.

"Very much."

He reached over then and brushed her thick hair back off her face. Then he kissed her lightly on the lips. "Tell me something, Ti," he said, "where is everybody?"

"What do you mean?"

"This town. Celestial City. What is it here for? On the road coming here we passed no one else. There were no signposts. And now that we're here, there is no railroad, no farmers nearby to make use of its stores, no traffic in or out of the town. If it were not for all your people, this would be a ghost town. I'll bet we're the first visitors this town has had in months."

"We do have visitors, Custis," she said sadly.

"Oh?"

"Those who come to take our people to work their mines."

"Would one of those visitors be a man called Malcolm Hartridge?"

"Yes," she said bitterly. "That is the one. But he is only the hireling of the one we truly fear."

"And who's that?"

"Dr. Fell."

Longarm frowned. This strange doctor seemed to be everywhere, a presence mysterious and malignant, hovering like a curse over these mountains. When Lotus had spoken of him, she had become quite uneasy, and the last words on Sharlow's lips spoke of this Dr. Fell.

"I've already heard about this jasper," Longarm told the girl. "Tell me more—all you know."

"His full name is Han Chow Fell."

"That I know already."

"He is called doctor because for many years he was a doctor in San Francisco. He is very well educated and lived for a while in England before returning here to enslave us."

"Enslave you? You mean in his silver mines?"

"Yes. There and in the mine we have here."

"I think maybe you better begin at the beginning."

She propped her head up on her palm. "Nearby," she told him, "we have found a very valuable mineral."

"Gold?"

"No. Jade."

"Jade?"

"Yes. We do not have to dig in the ground for it. It is found in streams, even on the ground in empty streambeds in large chunks."

"And you say this green rock is valuable to your people."

"It is more valuable than gold. We prize it as a gem stone. In our culture, a small piece of jade slipped under the tongue of a corpse before burial assures safe passage to the world of our ancestors."

"How does this fit in with Dr. Fell?"

"It is he who smuggles the jade back to China—for enormous profit, some of which he gives to his Tong, the rest to himself and this town."

"His Tong?"

"The Ong Leongs—the most powerful Tong in San Francisco."

"How does he get it all the way to China from here?"

"On the far side of the mountain there is a road our people have built. It goes over the mountains to California. There are also wagons and stables for the horses. There is a stamping mill there, too."

"How does Hartridge figure in this?"

"He works for Dr. Fell. He sees to it that his silver mines bring him much profit."

Then Hartridge, some time in the past, had made a deal with Dr. Fell. He had found out about the jade trade and his price for not interfering with it was silence, and part of the profits Dr. Fell realized from his silver mines. And meanwhile, of course, he was directed by the doctor to take from Celestial City as many coolies as he needed to run Dr. Fell's silver mines.

When Longarm told Ti what he had surmised, she agreed it made sense.

"And that means Dr. Fell owns this town and everyone in it."

"I am afraid so."

"Why don't you fight back? He's only one man."

"No, Custis. He is not only one man. He has many men. They owe allegiance only to him and will defend him to the death. There are those in our midst who listen closely to what we plan, then see to it that the doctor learns everything. Not a whisper, not a word goes unreported to him. At night his trained killers come like shadows and punish those who talk of fighting back or leaving this valley. We do not know who these informers are, so we live always in fear of Dr. Fell's terrible wrath."

Longarm shook his head. With informers in the town to warn him and a loyal, ruuhless cadre of hired killers and his personal bodyguard, no wonder the townsmen lived in terror.

"How many men does Fell have?" he asked.

"In his private bodyguard?"

"Yes."

"Twenty."

"That all?"

"Yes."

"Doesn't sound like such a large contingent," Longarm observed.

She shuddered. "You do not understand, Custis. These warriors are not like any men you have known. They kill with their feet or their hands. They are so strong, I have seen one of them smash through a porch post with a single blow from his hand."

Longarm sighed. "All right, I'm convinced. And I suppose your father and the rest of you dare not flee this town for fear of persecution, the kind you suffered in Denver."

"And every other place where my people have settled since arriving in San Francisco so many years ago."

"You have my sympathy, Ti."

"Thank you. But we do have hope."

"Oh?"

"Ling Chan has sent a delegation to Denver to speak with the owners of the Southern Pacific. If the owners of the railroad can be persuaded to send a rail link over the pass and through here, it would cut the travel time from Denver to San Francisco almost in half."

"But the pass is too high. In winter there would be no way a train could make it."

"Our people would build sheds to protect the tracks from avalanches. And we would provide the labor to lay the tracks too."

Longarm was impressed. "That should be a pretty good incentive."

"If our delegation succeeds, Celestial City will attract others, and soon it will become prosperous. Then we will be free of Dr. Fell."

"Does he know of this delegation?"

"We do not think so. But we do not know for sure. All of us are waiting and hoping."

"How long since the delegation left?"

"A month."

"You should have heard something by now."

She shrugged.

"Where is Dr. Fell?" he asked.

"He left some weeks ago for San Francisco with a jade shipment."

"Did he take that guard of his with him?"

"Yes."

"When do you expect him back?"

"Soon, I am afraid."

"When he hears about that delegation, he'll send his killers down here."

"I know."

"But this time Chan and the others are prepared to fight?"

She sighed. "We are always prepared to fight. But it does little good, I am afraid."

"Maybe this time it will be different."

"What do you mean?"

"I mean I think I'll hang around a mite longer and have a chat with the good doctor."

Startled, she sat up and looked at him. "You would do that? But why?"

"When I have all my clothes on, Ti, I am a deputy U. S. marshal. This here Dr. Fell is smuggling American precious metals to a foreign country. Maybe I could talk him into leaving the country for good."

"If you are a lawman, where is your badge?"

"I don't have it with me, but if I ever get to a telegraph office, I can have verification immediately. Now, tell me—where does Dr. Fell live when he is here?"

"Near his mine. It is a very fine house. Only a few of the townspeople have ever been inside it."

"Have you?"

"Yes." She dropped her eyes and glanced momentarily away, blushing.

"You don't need to explain."

"I was not intending to." She shuddered slightly. "Dr. Fell is a cold man. He has no soul. No woman could light a fire in such a man as he. I almost feel sorry for him."

"I feel sorry for your fellow townspeople."

She sighed. "We have done all we can."

"Maybe that delegation will come back with some good news."

"Yes, it is our only hope."

There was a long silence as Longarm contemplated the dilemma faced by the inhabitants of Celestial City. Trapped in a country whose citizens stoned them on sight, then burned their homes and places of business, they were now enslaved by one of their own people.

"Never mind," he told her at last, pulling her gently closer. "We can talk about it later." He kissed her on the lips and smiled. "Do you think it's possible maybe we could . . . ?"

She smiled slyly back at him. "Of course," she told him. "I have a few tricks up my sleeve yet. Just lean back and relax."

He did as she suggested. Reaching down, she found him and uttered a mock cry of pity that his manhood had shrunken to such a poor state. A moment later, her lips were rapidly improving the situation.

Chapter 9

Gunfire and sharp cries, followed by the clatter of horses in the street, awoke Longarm. He flung aside his covers and padded to the window.

Riders were tearing up and down the street, firing into the air, yelling out orders, doing all they could to terrorize the town's peaceful Chinese inhabitants. As some of them swept past the street lamps, Longarm thought he recognized a few of them. They were Hartridge's bully boys, come from the mine to requisition more slaves.

Protesting Chinese were being dragged into the main street, then hustled brutally toward a couple of high-backed ore wagons standing in the middle of it. Stationed there were two of Hartridge's men, who chained the rousted Chinese and forced them to clamber into the wagons.

As Longarm watched, he saw one Chinaman break away

from a small group being herded toward the wagons and make a run for it. He had almost reached an alley when one of Hartridge's riders overtook him and clubbed him to the ground with a truncheon. Leaving the coolie to be picked up by one of the men stationed at the ore wagons, the rider turned his mount and, laughing, went charging back up the street, looking for more targets of opportunity.

As he did so, a Chinaman stepped out of an alley and raised what appeared to be a bow of some kind. The shaft he sent after the rider looked smaller than an arrow and caught the rider in the side with such force the man was knocked clear off his horse. As he sprawled in the dust, another Chinaman standing on a roof let loose with a similar weapon. This time his missile did not strike its target, which was one of Hartridge's men in the act of herding two coolies toward the wagons. As the shaft hit the ground and bounded away, the gunman opened fire on the Chinaman, who toppled from the roof. At the same time, another rider roped from behind the other Chinaman, who dropped his bow and was dragged brutally down the street as other riders rode alongside, using the man as a target for their sixguns.

Longarm flung up his window sash, aimed carefully, and fired on the rider dragging the body. The rider sagged, then dropped off his horse. Longarm tracked another of the horsemen and fired, causing this one to yank his horse around suddenly, then topple to the ground.

The door opened behind Longarm as Charlie Fiddle and the others streamed into his room. He kept his attention on the street below his window and continued his firing at Hartridge's men.

"It's Hartridge!" Longarm told the others. "He's come for more coolies!"

The men had come away from the mine with no rifles and only Longarm's sixgun between them. Dancing in frustration at having no firepower to add to Longarm's gunplay, Charlie and the others watched as Longarm picked off two more horsemen. Then Longarm found himself out of ammunition.

"Let's get down there," Longarm drawled, tossing aside his empty weapon.

The four charged out of the room and out into the hotel porch. A few of the street lamps had ben shot out by now and in the darkness there was panic and confusion among the riders at what appeared to be a rapidly developing mutiny on the part of Celestial City's normally meek citizens.

Longarm saw a rider galloping toward him. Jumping from the porch, Longarm ran directly at the horse and rider, reaching up and catching the rider's arm as the man flashed by. Longarm was lifted from the ground, but the weight and fury of his charge was enough to drag the rider violently from his saddle. Both men hit the ground hard. The downed rider managed a blow to Longarm's chin, but Longarm shook it off and sent two crushing blows, a right and a left, into the man's face. His head snapped one way, then the other, and he lay quiet.

Longarm dragged the man's sixgun out of his holster, checked the load, then dropped it into his empty holster. The action had slowed suddenly, petering out almost as quickly as it had begun. Hartridge's riders had taken cover as a result of Longarm's earlier fusillade, while the chained Chinese were huddled close to the wagons for safety. Where Charlie, Burt, and Sanchez were at that moment, Longarm had no idea, but the night was filled with the sounds of running feet, sharp cries, and sporadic gunfire, which came from all about Longarm. He smiled. His three "deputies" had, like Longarm, managed to obtain weapons, and were putting them to use.

The horse belonging to the hardcase Longarm had just

dropped had pulled up near the hotel porch, his tail twitching nervously. Keeping low, Longarm overtook the horse, snaked the Winchester out of its saddle scabbard, and levered a fresh cartridge into its firing chamber just as a rider galloped into view. Longarm ducked behind a corner of the hotel porch and tracked the rider. Before he could get off a shot, however, the rider caught sight of Longarm and cut down an alley.

Longarm relaxed and peered about anxiously. He was looking for Hartridge. He had caught a glimpse of the man earlier, directing the raid from his horse in front of the mill. At the time, a cluster of riders had remained around him, preventing Longarm from getting a clear shot.

Peering in that direction now, Longarm saw no riders, and only an occasional darting figure. Longarm wondered how many of Hartridge's men were left. He had been able to count ten riders at least from the hotel window and he knew for certain that number that been cut considerably, perhaps in half. What Longarm was hoping for now was that Hartridge's losses would not be enough to cause him to cut and run. He wanted time to catch Hartridge in his Winchester's sights.

Burt darted from the mouth of an alley and dropped beside Longarm. "We got Hartridge!" he cried.

"Where?"

"Behind the livery. Charlie's got him pinned."

"Where's Sanchez?"

"I don't know. He's usin' his knife, so you won't hear much from him." Burt chuckled meanly. "Except for a scream every now and then."

"Let's go. I want Hartridge."

"Thought you'd say that." Burt grinned.

They darted across the street, then down a narrow back alley. Legging it past a couple of neat, picturesque privies, Longarm pulled up on a signal from Burt. Flattening himself against a wall, he waited for Burt to point out Charlie's position.

From behind a privy a few feet ahead of him, a rifle crashed. Charlie Fiddle's high voice cut through the night: "Raise your head a little higher, you son of a bitch, and I'll blow it off!"

Burt beckoned to Longarm. The two men slipped in behind the outhouse and found Charlie Fiddle crouched with a rifle behind an overturned barrel, a grin on his face.

"Where is the son of a bitch?" Longarm asked.

"A couple of feet from the stable doorway. I got him pinned. Him and one of his flunkies. Every time they make a break for the livery, I shave them with a round."

"We'll spread out," Longarm said. "Take him from two sides."

"Good idea," said Charlie. "I'm runnin' low on shells."

"I wish we could take him alive," muttered Burt, as he followed after Longarm through the darkness. "I want to hear that bastard squeal."

Longarm did not answer. He found a corral fence and settled behind it. From this vantage point he could see the entire rear entrance. A lantern was glowing from inside the stable, spilling enough light out onto the back alley to outline Hartridge clearly the moment he broke for the stable.

Longarm waited.

The shadows beside the doorway grew larger. There was a slight scuffle, it seemed, and someone—not Hartridge—darted for the entrance. Longarm wanted Hartridge, so he let the man go. As the fellow disappeared into the stable, Hartridge decided it was safe and darted after him. Longarm tracked him swiftly and fired.

Hartridge's hat went flying. Longarm cursed, levered, and fired again, but Hartridge had disappeared into the barn. Still cursing, Longarm clambered over the fence and darted into the barn. Burt and Charlie pounded in after him. Hartridge was nowhere in sight, and before they could find cover, a gun spoke from the loft over their heads, narrowly missing Longarm.

The three men dove for cover, firing up at the loft as they did so.

"Shit," said Burt. "Now *we're* the targets."

Longarm saw Hartridge's head lift up from behind the side of a stall and punched a shot at him. Hartridge ducked back down out of sight.

"Keep me covered," Longarm said.

As Burt and Charlie kept a steady fire on the gunslick in the loft, Longarm darted toward the stall Hartridge was using for cover. Before he reached it, Hartridge stood up quickly and fired at Longarm. The bullet caught Longarm's heel. His foot went flying, and Longarm found himself sprawling face up on the barn floor. Hartridge surged out of the stall and headed for the front entrance. Rolling over as quickly as he could, Longarm sighted and fired, but Hartridge vanished into the night.

Longarm got to his feet and hobbled toward the barn entrance. A second before he reached it, he heard the clatter of a horse, and Hartridge calling to his men. Longarm stepped out into the street in time to see Hartridge and the remainder of his riders galloping out of town. A second later, he heard the sudden thunder of their hoofs as they crossed the bridge.

From the loft above Longarm came a high, piercing scream.

Longarm spun and raced back into the barn in time to see Hartridge's companion come hurtling from the loft. With a sickening thud, he hit the solid floor face down, moved just once, then lay still. A knife was buried up to its hilt in his back. With a wave, Sanchez stepped onto a beam high above them, his face radiating the satisfaction he felt.

A moment later Sanchez dropped lightly to the barn floor. Striding over to the man he had just killed, he withdrew his knife and wiped the blade clean on his sleeve. "This cockroach, I know," he told them. "He like to call me a stupid. Sometimes he say I am unwashed greaser. And all the time I see him suck around Hartridge like a dog in heat." He chuckled. "Now he is only dead gringo with wet pants. Hey! Where is Hartridge?"

"He got away," Longarm told him.

Charlie Fiddle glanced down at Longarm's foot. "You all right?" he asked.

"Hartridge's slug caught my boot heel. No harm done," he said.

At that moment, the four men became aware of a large and growing body of silent Chinese materializing out of the night. Ling Chan was at their head. Some of the Chinese behind him, Longarm noticed, were still wearing the iron collars Hartridge's men had clamped about their necks a few minutes before.

"Looks like we got visitors," Charlie commented.

"Do not be afraid," Ling Chan called in to them.

"We ain't," responded Longarm.

Ling Chan stopped in the livery doorway and bowed to Longarm. "A kind Providence has sent you four brave men to us. We hope you will stay as our guests."

"No need to thank us," said Longarm. "We had a score of our own to settle with them bastards."

"If that is so, we thank you all the same."

"Do you mind if I ask you a question?" Longarm asked.

"Ask anything you wish."

"Why in blazes don't you people get together and defend yourselves?"

"Defend ourselves?"

"Yes."

"And how do you propose we do such a thing?"

"Get yourselves organized. Form a militia of some kind."

Ling Chan smiled and bowed in deference. "If you will

forgive me," he said, "but the arts of war are not those we have mastered. Unlike our honored guests, we are not Lords of War."

Longarm shrugged wearily. Hartridge would return with more men—and, if that didn't work, Dr. Fell would lay his heavy hand upon these poor, frightened villagers. Men had to be willing to fight for their freedom if they were to have any.

Longarm bid goodnight to Ling Chang, left the livery, and started for the hotel across the street. The crowd of silent Chinamen parted silently and most respectfully for the four Lords of War.

The next afternoon, resplendent in his new brown tweed suit—a suit the tailor must have worked through a very wild night to produce—Longarm rejoined Charlie and the others on the hotel porch. He had bought a black Stetson from the store Chou Li-Fan had recommended, and though he didn't particularly like the color, it was the only hat he could find to fit him. So long had it been on the shelf, in fact, that it had taken a considerable length of time for the store owner to clean it properly. There were just not that many customers passing through Celestial City looking for headgear.

At his approach, the three men hooted and whistled merrily. When they finished inspecting his suit from pants cuffs to collar, they demanded that he lead the way to the saloon and stand them all to some tonsil varnish. Longarm agreed readily, and the four men marched in to the saloon.

Something they had all noticed the day before, and even more so this morning, was the lack of usage the saloon was put in this town. It was a fine-looking establishment, but it resembled more a museum than a working saloon with its highly polished woodwork and long mahogany bar, the immaculate mirror that ran the length of the wall behind it, the tables and chairs neatly set out, the fresh sawdust on the floor, and the brass cuspidors polished to a high gloss.

"Select a table, gents," said Longarm. "Just ignore the crowd."

"Yeah, I noticed," said Burt. "How come this place is so deserted?"

Charlie chuckled. "The Celestials have their own amusements and their own places of amusement. I noticed an alley last night that got pretty heavy traffic until well after midnight. It led to a cellar in back."

"What they got for sale in there?"

"Opium, I imagine. That's their way of relaxin'. They prefer it to hard liquor."

Sanchez shrugged. "Every man to his own poison, I alway say."

The three left Longarm at the bar and found a table in the back. Longarm asked for two bottles of rye, but when he slapped a couple of gold coins down on the bar in payment, the barkeep—a little bald Chinaman with a face as wrinkled as a prune—would not take his money and backed hastily away, shaking his head all the while. He acted as if Longarm's attempt to pay was some kind of indiscretion.

Lugging the two bottles and the glasses over to his companions' table, Longarm sat down, his eyebrows still raised. "Any of you notice that?"

"Notice what?" Burt asked, reaching for one of the bottles.

"Our money's no good here."

"What money? I don't have any money."

"If you did, it wouldn't be any good. Nowhere in this town. When the blacksmith pulled that slug out of my boot this morning, he refused payment. Later, when I tried to pay the tailor for my suit here a little while ago, he wouldn't take any money. And just now that barkeep wouldn't let me pay for this liquor."

"Well, well, well," mused Charlie happily as he poured himself a shot. "Ain't that a goddamn shame. I think maybe I could get to like this town."

"We're heroes," said Burt, chucking his hat back off his forehead and grinning around at his companions. "They figure they owe us for last night. They're givin' us the key to Celestial City."

"Hah, that is nothing, I tell you," said Sanchez. "They ain't nothin' here, *amigos*. Never have I seen such a dead town."

They all recognized the truth of that statement. It sobered them, and for a moment the three men drank silently, intently, the little Chinese barkeep peering over the bar at them with wide eyes.

"Say, Longarm," said Charlie, "do you suppose if we're such big shots, maybe they'll show us where this here gold mine of theirs is."

"There's no gold mine, Charlie," said Longarm.

"What do you mean?" cried Burt. "Look at this place! What else could be keeping this town going?"

"I told you," repeated Longarm. "There's no gold. That ain't what's doin' it."

"Then what is?"

"Jade."

Burt squinted at Longarm. "Jade? What in the hell is that?"

"A precious stone these Chinese put great store by. The thing is, it's being smuggled back to China, where it's worth something—and that's where the money's comin' from to keep this place alive."

Charlie squinted unhappily at Longarm. "Would you mind goin' over that a mite slower?"

Longarm pulled his chair closer and told them what he had learned from Ti-Ling the evening before about Dr. Fell and his reasons for financing Celestial City. When Longarm had finished, his three companions leaned back in their chairs with puzzled, unhappy looks on their faces as they digested what he had told them.

Burt was the first to speak. "Poor sons of bitches. These coolies're forced to work for Hartridge—and this oriental son of a bitch, too. They're getting reamed from both sides."

"That's why we don't see no piles of ore or hear no mills banging away to crush it," said Charlie unhappily. "They just pick this stuff out of the streams, clean it up a little, and let this Dr. Fell ship it over the mountains to California. That it?"

Longarm reached for the bottle and nodded. "That's what I been told."

"Where's this Dr. Fell now?"

"He's taking a shipment to California."

"This here sure sounds crazy," said Burt.

"That's right, *amigos,*" said Sanchez, pouring himself another drink, "crazy enough to be true. So I think maybe we better get out of here."

Charlie chuckled and downed his drink. "What's the hurry?" he asked, reaching for the bottle. "Long as these here slants keep our glasses and bellies full."

At that moment the batwings swung open as Ling Chan and two younger Chinese entered the bar and walked toward them. The four men put down their drinks and waited. When the three orientals reached their table, they halted, then bowed. It was like a stage show.

"We are most sorry to disturb honorable guests," Ling Chan said.

"Forget it," said Longarm. "What do you want?"

"Many weeks ago we send a delegation to Denver to speak with owners of Southern Pacific Railroad. We want the masters of the Southern Pacific to build railroad through here. We offer to help them. We think then maybe we can live without fear of this man Hartridge."

"And Dr. Fell," Longarm added.

Ling Chan was startled. "You . . . know of him."

Longarm indicated his three companions with a wave of his hand. "We all do. And we know about the jade, too."

"I see." Ling Chan thought about that for a moment, then continued his story. "Very early this morning, one of those men we send to Denver come back. He was wounded very bad and die soon after he get here."

"I'm sorry to hear that, Ling Chan. Did he get to Denver?"

Ling Chan shook his head bitterly. "He and the rest of delegation were caught by Hartridge before they reach Green's Creek. All this time they work in one of his silver mine. Now they all dead."

"Sorry, Ling Chan."

"But that is not why I have come here to speak to you."

Longarm moved a bottle aside so his view of Ling Chan was unobstructed. "Go on, Ling Chan."

"Last night you say we should fight."

"That's what I said."

"But Hartridge and Dr. Fell have much wealth, and many armed men who ride for them."

"You can take them. There's that marshland Hartridge's men've got to cross to get here, and then there's that mountain flank at your back, so they can't cut you off. If you fight hard enough and skillfully enough, you can outlast them. And this Dr. Fell is only one man."

"Perhaps. Many have say what you say."

Longarm shrugged. "Then fight."

"Did you not say last night we must make militia first?"

Longarm nodded.

"But what is this militia?"

"Local citizens organized into a fighting unit to protect their land and their people. Says in the Constitution you got a right to bear arms to protect yourself."

"I do not know about this constitution. But how we make militia?"

"Organize yourselves. Elect a leader, someone to train and drill you. Arm yourselves. Then prepare to fight."

Ling Chan smiled and tipped his head ingratiatingly. "As I think I say last night, the arts of war are not those your humble servants have mastered. But, fortunately, such is not the case with you four Lords of Battle. Is that not so?"

Longarm saw where this was leading. "Sure. We know how to handle ourselves in a scrap."

"Then will you help us make this militia? Many of our people want to fight these men."

"Now you done it," said Sanchez. "Jesus, Longarm. You got these poor slants all fired up for nothing. Hell, how they goin' to fight? They don't have no weapons. There's not a store in this place carries a firearm. I went lookin' this morning."

"That's right," chimed in Charlie Fiddle. "These poor fellers in their black pajamas can't use bare hands against rifles and sidearms."

Longarm nodded wearily and looked back at Ling Chan. "Your people need firearms," he told him, "weapons to fight with. Do you have any stashed away?"

"We have no guns and we have no rifles. Dr. Fell does not allow us to have such weapons." Having said that, Ling Chan took a small step forward, his face brightening. "But we do have other weapons."

"Maybe he's thinkin' of firecrackers," Burt whispered to Longarm.

"What other weapons?" Longarm asked Ling Chan.

"Crossbows. The ancient weapon of our people."

Longarm remembered then the two Chinese he had seen firing on Hartridge's men with small, bowlike weapons. He leaned suddenly closer. "Your people have crossbows?"

Ling Chan turned to the young Chinese next to him. The

fellow took a step closer and bowed stiffly. "I have build many," he told Longarm.

"Didn't I see some of your townsmen using them last night?"

"Yes."

"How many of Hartridge's men did you cut down?"

"Only one."

"Well, that's something. I think maybe we'd like to see one of those crossbows."

The young man turned to Ling Chan for permission to leave. Ling Chan nodded quickly. At once the fellow darted from the place.

"Guess we'll just have to sit back and relax," Longarm drawled, pouring himself a drink.

The others did likewise. A short time later, carrying a crossbow and a couple of bolts, the young Chinaman hurried back into the saloon. As he handed the crossbow and the bolts across the table to Longarm, Ling Chan spoke up.

"This is Tai Wong and his friend, Wan San. Tai Wong is the one who make crossbow. Wan San, he make bolts."

Longarm nodded to the two men, then carefully examined the crossbow as the others, just as curious, got hastily out of their chairs to peer over his shoulder at it.

The firing mechanism was simple enough: a claw sitting on the same pin as the trigger held the drawn string in place. Pulling back on the trigger lowered the claw, releasing the string and the bolt. The trigger mechanism appeared to have an intermediate part so that the slightest tug on the trigger was sufficient to release the string. There was a notch in the stock to hold the bolt in place, and the bow itself was ash reinforced with sinew. Since there were no gears or any other mechanism for pulling back the string, and no stirrup, the one using it would have to stand on the center of the bow and haul the string back manually until it engaged the claw.

"Here. Let me see if I can pull that string back," Burt said, reaching for the crossbow.

Longarm handed it to Burt. As soon as he saw how easy it was for Burt to draw the string back over the claw, he turned his attention to the bolts Wan San had fashioned. They seemed solid enough and true. The vanes were of wood and expertly fletched to the shaft. Longarm had seen others like these once in a museum. But this was the first really close look at a true crossbow and its bolts he had ever had. Though this weapon of Tai Wong and Wan San was not much more than a crude copy of those elaborate weapons he had seen earlier, there was no doubt in his mind that this crossbow could be just as effective in the right hands.

Longarm looked at Tai Wong. "How many of these do you have?"

"Many! Ten now. But I can build more. Quickly."

Longarm glanced around at his companions. "Well, gents," he said, reaching out to take the crossbow back from Burt, who seemed thoroughly fascinated by it, "that should be enough for us to stop Hartridge, I reckon—and this Dr. Fell too, while we're at it."

"We?" cried Burt.

"Now, just a doggone minute," drawled Charlie.

"Burt," Longarm went on, "I figure you could handle training the coolies to use the crossbow. Charlie could take care of formations and tactics and military discipline." Longarm glanced at Sanchez. "Sanchez, you might see to their night-fighting talents, the quiet and efficient use of stealth, for instance—and knives."

Sanchez appeared to be ready to protest until he glanced at Charlie Fiddle and Burt and saw the eager light in their eyes.

"This is crazy, *amigos,*" he protested lightly. "But, if I can be of some small help . . ."

"Fine," said Longarm, getting to his feet and handing the crossbow back to Tai Wong and the two bolts back to Wan San. "I declare this council of war adjourned. It looks, gents, like we're going to be building ourselves an army."

Chapter 10

A week later, with Charlie and the others off on the other side of the marshland drilling their Chinese militia, Longarm and Ti saddled horses and rode out to reconnoitre Dr. Fell's jade mine. Ling Chan had confided to Longarm his fear that the tyrant was due to return soon from California.

Ling Chan had agreed that Ti-Ling would be the best guide for Longarm, and as they rode out, the Chinaman who had sold Longarm his black Stetson pressed upon him a battered pair of binoculars. Though the townspeople hated Hartridge violently, it was Dr. Fell they feared the most, with an intensity bordering on hysteria. An awareness of the fateful course the townspeople were now taking had put everyone on edge. As Longarm and Ti rode past them out of town, some citizens bowed so low their foreheads seemed to brush the earth.

It was a long climb to the pass leading over the mountain, and about mid-afternoon Ti and Longarm pulled their mounts to a halt on a ridge which gave them an unobstructed view of the sparse, pine-stippled flat below them. Across its nearer edge, almost directly below, sprawled the buildings comprising Dr. Fell's mining operation.

Grateful for the binoculars, Longarm surveyed the site. There were at least four barns for the horses and corrals and crude log bins where the jade ore was kept before it was loaded into the ore wagons. High-sided wagons were lined up neatly before the chutes, and the stamping mill, which had been built alongside a stream, was apparently being powered by water power, its steady thump a far cry from the earth-shaking pounding of the mill atop the shaft of Hartridge's silver mine.

As Longarm studied the layout, he could hear the steady clangor of the blacksmith and saw many Chinese moving about among the buildings. Behind the stables, a wrangler was herding back into the main corral a small bunch of work horses. The wrangler, a Chinaman, looked oddly out of place on the horse, dressed as he was in his black silk pajamas, and wearing a conical hat instead of the usual wide-brimmed Stetson. Still, the wrangler sat his horse with the same easy skill as any Texas-born horseman and seemed to be doing a perfectly creditable job.

"Where's Dr. Fell's house?" Longarm asked.

"Up there," Ti said.

She was pointing to a clump of pine on the other side of the valley. The clump was higher than they were, across the valley on a flank of the mountain facing them. Longarm trained his binoculars on the pines, adjusted the lens, and caught through them the peculiar sloping roof favored by the Chinese, along with the smooth, whitewashed sides of what appeared to be a mansion. Studying it more closely, he saw that the rear of the building was built into the side of the mountain.

Lowering his binoculars, he looked at Ti. "Very impressive. It would take an army to storm that place."

"Yes," she agreed, her voice small.

Glancing back down at the mine buildings, Longarm said, "I don't see many miners about."

"It is early yet," Ti explained. "They are still off searching for the jade."

"How far do they have to go?"

"Great distances. They seek out gullies, the beds of streams, dry washes. They look everywhere for the green stones that other miners years before flung aside as worthless. When they find these stones or pieces of jade, they drop them into the wheelbarrows they have taken with them. Then they push them all the way back here and dump them into those bins."

"Doesn't sound like a very pleasant job."

"From dawn to dusk they work, Custis. I came up here once to find my father. When I saw how hard he labored, I began to cry. He was fifty-six then. I am very grateful to Dr. Fell that he is no longer forced to mine the jade."

"That was when you visited Dr. Fell?"

She looked at him. "Yes. And I would do the same thing again if I had to."

"You don't need to explain to me. Does your father know?"

"He has not spoken of it. Perhaps he knows. But he says nothing."

"I am sure he is very grateful."

She shrugged. "It does not matter. I did what I had to do."

"What happens when Dr. Fell comes back?"

"If you are asking, will he send for me again, the answer

is he may, unless he has brought back a new woman from San Francisco."

"And will you go if he sends for you?"

She looked at him. "If I have no choice."

Longarm glanced back at Dr. Fell's operation. "I'd like to get closer, give this place a real looking-over. I got a hunch there's going to be some tough fighting around here before long."

With a shrug, Ti pulled her mount back off the ledge, then led Longarm down through the close-packed pines until they found an open spot at the edge of the timber only a few hundred yards above the flat.

Longarm and Ti dismounted. Ti took the reins of both mounts and kept beside Longarm while he positioned himself with his back to a pine and began sweeping the flat with the binoculars, studying closely the two barrack-like log buildings that apparently housed those coolies who were forced to remain up here. A much more substantial building fronted the clearing. This one had solid chimneys and a porch, and like Dr. Fell's stronghold above, it too was built into the flanks of the mountain. From the solidity of its construction, Longarm decided this might well be the quarters of the men who were running the mine for Dr. Fell.

Two white men strode out onto the veranda. They had bottles in their hands and were smoking cigars. Longarm watched one of them toss his cigar stub off the porch and turn to his friend, his beefy face creased in silent laughter. His sagging mid-section, Longarm did not fail to notice, was cut by a broad gunbelt.

Longarm swept the binoculars past the two men and focused next on a large cookshack and after that on the stables beyond. Closer to him he saw a blacksmith shop and a livery stable. For a moment he glimpsed a flock of Rhode Island Red chickens roaming loose behind a henhouse, and he caught a momentary glimpse of two Chinese cooks lugging water to the cookshack.

He was focusing in on the high-backed ore wagons when Ti gasped and nudged him. Lowering his binoculars, he saw her peering westward at a high, narrow pass.

"Dr. Fell!" she cried. "He is back!"

Longarm lifted his glasses and focused them on a small caravan escorted by quite a few riders, with a black coach at its center.

"Fine," Longarm said. "It's about time I got a look at the son of a bitch."

"We must get higher," she told him. "We are too close now. If he sees us, he will come after us!"

Longarm started to protest, but the alarm in Ti's voice prompted him to go along with her plea. They remounted and rode back up through the pines to the ridge from which they had first viewed the flat. By that time Dr. Fell's entourage was in full view, heading straight for the mine.

Longarm lifted the binoculars. The coach was drawn by a team of four powerful black horses and was painted a gleaming black with silver trim about the doors and windows and on the wheels' spokes. The lamps and other fixtures, including the driver's seat, were also trimmed in silver. Once or twice the sun glinted off the polished black sides of the coach, momentarily blinding Longarm. Beside the driver sat a Chinese guard carrying a shotgun. The top of the wagon was surmounted by a high railing, within which many large trunks were secured with broad straps.

Carefully adjusting the binoculars, Longarm kept them trained on the two side windows and was able to focus finally on the lean, ascetic face of a Chinese gentleman in a bowler hat, a man of indeterminate age with high cheekbones, emerald eyes, and a thin mustache across his upper lip which descended into a sharp, well-trimmed beard covering his chin. A moment later, as the stage rocked closer, he peered into the other window and glimpsed two women sitting across from Dr. Fell. One of them was breathtakingly beautiful, her complexion the color of polished ebony. The other was a blonde, equally beautiful, her eyes—for a moment she gazed straight into the binoculars—a deep lake-blue.

It did not appear that Dr. Fell would be requiring the services of Ti-Ling this evening.

He shifted his attention to Dr. Fell's bodyguard. The guard riding on the seat beside the driver and those that made up the doctor's mounted escort were all dressed similarly in long black tunics and trousers, their seams trimmed in silver. For headgear they wore the traditional Chinese conical hats, also black. The doctor's guards rode with rifles slung over their shoulders and, to Longarm's surprise, sabers at their sides.

In addition to the two escorts who rode close to the wagon, one on each side, there were four more mounted guards in front—two at a point well ahead of the wagon, and two more just in front of the horses. At the rear there were four more riding drag, two on each side of the wagon. Sweeping his binoculars to the left and right of the wagon, Longarm glimpsed one rider below him on the flat and another one clear on the other side, moving up into the timbered slope.

"I count twelve guards, so far," Longarm told Ti. "You said there were twenty."

"You cannot see the others," she told him. "They follow in the hills, watching." She shuddered. "Some of his guards could be in those pines below us even now."

Longarm nodded. That sure as hell made sense. Such a tactic would keep some members of Dr. Fell's escort out of sight, ready to pounce on any attacking force that might strike at his coach. This Dr. Fell took no chances, it seemed.

"Let's go," Longarm said to Ti. "I've seen enough for now."

• • •

They were approaching the pass, just emerging from a clump of aspen, when the attack came. Two mounted Chinese warriors, sabers flashing, bore down on them from opposite sides. Longarm only had time to wheel his horse and draw his sixgun before the first of the two attackers reached him, his horse slamming into Longarm's, knocking him from his saddle.

As Longarm hit the tall grass on his back, he looked up to see the black-garbed Chinamen leaping to the ground beside him. Thumbcocking and firing in almost the same motion, he saw something black and powerful smash into the chest of his attacker. The pajama-clad warrior had been holding his saber over his head. He let it go and sank to the ground.

Longarm jumped to his feet just as Ti screamed. He looked over and saw the other rider hauling her aboard his horse. Bringing up his revolver, he tracked the galloping rider, but dared not fire for fear of striking Ti. He snatched the trailing reins of his own mount, swung up into his saddle, and galloped after Ti. He was crossing a short grassy stretch when he saw four other riders breaking from the pines in front of the fleeing rider.

He hauled up hastily, wheeled his horse, and rode back the way he had come. Ti was alive—Dr. Fell's captive. And that was too bad. But, after all, he told himself gloomily, it was not as if she were entirely unacquainted with the man.

When Longarm brought the grim news of Ti's capture by one of Dr. Fell's men to her father, Chou Li-Fan bowed his head suddenly. Clasping his hands before him, he wheeled and disappeared behind the curtained doorway, where he might grieve in solitude.

Longarm left the tailor's shop and hurried to the saloon,

where the others were waiting. It was well past sundown, and much had to be done. If Ti was sensible, she would tell Dr. Fell everything he wanted to know. And that, coupled with the news his informers would bring him, would bring the full might of Dr. Fell's wrath down upon the rebellious citizens of the Celestial City.

Charlie Fiddle, Burt, and Sanchez were waiting in the saloon along with Ling Chan, Tai Wong, and Wan San. In addition, there were two other powerful-looking Chinese of middle age, who now figured prominently in the militia Longarm and his men had been laboring to whip into shape this past week.

Tables had been shoved together. As soon as Longarm sat down and filled his glass, Charlie Fiddle cleared his throat.

"We've already sent out patrols," he said.

"Armed?"

"Yes."

"Good idea."

"Do you think he'll attack tonight?" Burt asked.

"No."

"Why not?" asked Sanchez.

"He has just completed a long journey. He has quite a bit to absorb all at once. This is the first real challenge to his authority. He'll want to organize things, maybe even get in touch with Hartridge."

"We don't want that," said Charlie.

"So what do we do? Wait him out?" asked Sanchez.

Longarm glanced over at Ling Chan. "What do you say, Ling?"

"We must wait. Prepare!"

"What about you, Tai Wong—and you, Wan San. Do you agree we should wait and prepare for Dr. Fell's attack?"

Both men shook their heads vigorously. It was Tai Wong who spoke. "We must not wait."

"You mean attack now?"

"Yes," said Wan San. "Now is good time."

"What about you, Charlie?"

"I hate to go messin' around in the dark. But we've been practicin' all week. Might as well have a go at it."

Longarm glanced at Burt and Sanchez. They both nodded in agreement.

Longarm leaned back in his chair. "Then that's settled. We attack tonight. Before Dr. Fell gets his feet under him."

"You got any ideas, Longarm?" Charlie drawled.

"Sure. We move out now. If we leave soon enough, we should be at the mine site a little before midnight. We take the place. Free the miners, then move up the mountain to the doctor's mansion. It won't be easy, and I sure as hell hope Tai Wong and Wan San's crossbows can do the job."

"One thing's for sure," said Sanchez, running his blade through the hairs on his arm. "Them bolts are as silent as my knife. Should be one very interesting night."

Longarm got to his feet. "All right, Charlie. I'm saddle-sore and hungry, but we'll be moving out in a few hours. Call your militia together. I'll be ready to ride when you are."

While Longarm stayed back with Sanchez, Charlie and Burt led their men across the flat and onto the mine site. In a moment they had disappeared into the shadows of the ore wagons. Longarm and Sanchez waited silently, their own ten-man crossbow teams crouched behind them in the grass.

There were enough horses to go around, but not enough crossbows, not yet. Accordingly, the Celestials were trained to ride to a fight, but, like the U. S. Cavalry, to dismount when doing battle. Since loading a crossbow was a difficult feat, there were two men to a bow, one to fire and one to load. It was Charlie's idea to divide the militia into ten-man teams, each with five crossbowmen, the ten-man group corresponding to an army platoon, with two ten-man teams making up a company. So far, in mock skirmishes, it had worked fine.

Now they were to test their skills in real combat.

The battle plan was for Burt's assault group to invest the building where those guarding the miners slept, with Charlie's men taking out any guards that might be stationed outside the coolies' sleeping quarters, then freeing the coolies, after which Longarm and Sanchez would move in to mop up and join the assault on the stronghold—what they had come to call Dr. Fell's mansion.

A shot rang out. Then came a cry. After that, silence. A door opened in one of the buildings—the guards' quarters. Light streamed out from behind the one standing in the doorway. There was no shot, but the man crumpled suddenly in the doorway, and a moment later a stream of men scrambled out into the darkness. There were muffled cries, a few groans, then silence. The crossbowmen were doing their deadly work well.

Another door opened, flooding the ground near one of the barns with light, and more men hurried into the night. Abruptly, firing broke out. This time it was steady. Longarm and Sanchez got up and hurried across the flat, their crossbow teams right behind them.

As soon as they reached the mine area, Longarm halted and motioned for his crossbowmen to spread out. They vanished into the darkness, Sanchez with them. The door to the guards' quarters was still open. Longarm headed for the building and was halfway up the steps when a guard appeared out of nowhere, a bolt protruding from his chest. The man loomed helplessly above Longarm, then toppled down the stairs past him.

Longarm darted into the building and found himself in a long, barrack-like room, cots lining both walls. At the far end loomed a great stone fireplace. He ran to a doorway beside it and was stepping through it into a narrow, chamber-like room when a portion of the opposite wall swung silently open and two of Dr. Fell's bodyguards stepped through it.

Pulling up in astonishment, Longarm fired first at the nearest guard, and then at the other. The first one sagged to the floor, while the other, with amazing dexterity, flung his saber at Longarm. Longarm ducked, but the point of the saber caught his sleeve, pinning his right arm to the doorjamb.

In the instant it took Longarm to pull himself free of the saber, the second guard was on him. With lightning-like speed his foot lashed out, his heel catching Longarm's chin, smashing his head back against the wall. Longarm tried to ward off the next blow, but another amazing kick, this one to his neck, caused Longarm to gasp for breath. Another blow, this one to Longarm's mid-section, cut Longarm down cruelly, and he found himself slipping down the wall to the floor.

Only dimly was he aware of the guard looming over him—and of the seeping hole in the man's chest. Sagging crookedly, the guard slumped to the floor beside Longarm. Longarm crawled over to him. In addition to his black pajamas, the guard had a silver sash wound about his waist with a sixgun stuck into it. Pulling the weapon free, Longarm broke open the cylinder. It was fully loaded. Casting aside his now empty revolver, Longarm dropped the guard's sixgun into his holster and began searching through the man's pockets for more bullets.

He found instead a large brass key. His head clearer now, he scrambled to his feet and hurried over to the wall, looking for a way through it. The light was dim, and no matter how closely he peered at the wall's rough stone surface, he could find no indication of a break. He began feeling the wall, hoping to come upon a hidden lever, when he heard a slight scratching sound coming from behind the wall.

He stepped swiftly to one side as once again the hidden door swung open. The single guard who stepped into the passageway did not look to his right or left as he stared down instead at the two bodies sprawled on the floor in front of him. Longarm clubbed him unconscious with one vicious swipe from his sixgun, then jammed the gun barrel into the crack of the door before it swung shut entirely.

Grabbing the edge of the opening with one hand, he hauled back on the door, aware that he was working against very heavy weights. Gradually the door opened wide enough for him to slip through. Once he was safely on the other side, the door slammed shut behind him. Longarm found himself staring up at a long flight of steps fashioned out of railroad ties and set into the side of the mountain. The steps were dimly lit by smudged oil lamps set into niches cut into the passageway's walls.

He paused a moment, listening for any more of Dr. Fell's guards, then ran up the stairs. He soon found himself struggling to catch his breath. As he paused to do so, he realized why he was so exhausted. The stairs were leading almost straight up at better than a forty-five-degree angle.

He took it somewhat easier for the rest of the climb. At the top of the stairway, he was faced with a large door. But this one had a lock. He took out the key he had taken from the guard and inserted it. The key turned easily and he heard the door's lock click open.

Carefully, he eased the door back and stepped through into a long hallway. The door clicked shut behind him. He glanced back at it and found it had disappeared, so closely did it fit into the wall. He turned back around. There were no windows in the hallway, and the only light came from kerosene lamps fastened to the walls. Their shafts were fitted with red globes, which sent a dim red light over the walls and the thick red carpeting underneath.

The floor of the hallway sloped up at a gentle angle,

causing Longarm to assume he was still inside the mountain, moving through the last passage leading into the mansion itself. On the walls hung exquisite Chinese paintings and tapestries, most of which portrayed mist-covered mountain slopes or brilliantly plumed dragons rearing up to do battle.

He turned a corner. A heavily draped wall stood before him. Pushing aside the drapes, he found himself facing still another door, this one equipped with a simple doorknob. Longarm turned it and carefully pushed open the door. The corridor it led into was dimly lit, the walls covered with more black satin drapes. Unholstering the sixgun he had taken from the guard, he slipped into the room and closed the door softly behind him. There was a red paneled door to his right, another to his left, and a larger door straight ahead on the opposite wall.

This one also was painted black, with silver trim around the panels.

Beyond that doorway, Longarm knew, was Dr. Fell.

Then he heard something—voices, or someone crying out; he couldn't be sure which. It was coming from behind the door to his left. He pulled the door open and saw a spiral staircase leading straight down. He closed the door behind him and plunged into Stygian darkness. Pulling up after a while, he listened intently.

Yes. Those were voices he heard, coming from far below.

He descended swiftly and found himself passing a narrow, barred window. He paused and glanced out. Bathed in weak moonlight, a stand of pines sloped steeply down the mountainside away from Dr. Fell's mansion. Then, as he watched, Longarm caught sight of men struggling up the slope through the pines, while Dr. Fell's black-garbed warriors poured down the slope to meet them. The faint rattle of gunfire came to him through the window.

Longarm continued on down the staircase and came at last to a dimly lit passageway crowded with wooden buckets and a barrel of kerosene. Farther on, past the kerosene, sat a large wooden barrel. Glancing into it, Longarm saw it was piled high with a moist accumulation of human waste. The stench of it was like a kick to his mid-section. As he hurried on past it, a rat scurried away, its feet scuttling faintly.

At the end of the passageway, Longarm came to a huge oak door. It was slightly ajar. He slipped through and found himself in a long corridor, on both sides of which were iron doors leading to cells. The only light came from dim kerosene lamps set in niches in the walls.

In the center of the room there was a chair with manacles attached to the broad arm rests and two additional manacles on the floor, adjacent to the spot where a victim's feet would be resting. High on the back of the chair was a collar and pads and leather straps used to hold fast the victim's head. Longarm could see in his mind's eye the poor wretches who over the years had found themselves strapped in this chair while Dr. Fell's brutes went to work on them. Surrounding the chair, Longarm noticed, were large stains of blood.

A groan came from one cell. Longarm holstered his gun and lifted down one of the kerosene lamps. Hurrying over to the cell, he held the lantern close up to the tiny, barred window and peered in. What he glimpsed sickened him: a coolie, beaten so ruthlessly it was difficult for Longarm to realize that what he saw huddled in a corner on a pile of his own filth was a human being. Longarm became aware of faint, agitated squeaking sounds. Moving the lantern again slightly, he saw a swarm of sleek rats darting quickly over the coolie's body.

Longarm pulled away in horror. He had no key to the cell. And even if he did, what chance would that near-dead creature in there have now? With mounting anger, Longarm continued on until he reached a short stairway which led to a narrow landing. He pushed another door open and found himself in a dim anteroom. The only light came from a crack under a door on its far side.

He paused, suddenly alert.

Beyond the door he heard voices—the same voices that had drawn him down into this dungeon. Standing there, Longarm became aware of a sweet, cloying smell. Opium. Then he heard laughter and knew at once what he would find when he opened the door. Putting the lantern down, he moved lightly across the anteroom and rested his ear against the panels.

The low murmur of a man's voice, powerful in timbre and used to command, came clearly through the door. Longarm had no doubt by this time that he was listening to Dr. Fell. The man was speaking in English, his voice seductive, coaxing. Then came the sudden, delighted cry of a woman's laughter, followed by the husky voice of still another woman. The second woman began uttering short, quickening grunts that sounded quite urgent.

Stepping back, Longarm took out his Colt, planted his foot squarely against the door alongside the knob, and kicked hard. The lock gave and the door swung wide.

Striding into the room, Longarm pulled up, astonished. He was in a spacious bedroom, its windowless walls covered with royal blue drapes, while the massive bed itself was enclosed in a spectacular red silk canopy. The air of the room was alive with shifting curtains of heavy blue smoke, through which it was difficult to see anything clearly, and it was this which lent such an air of unreality to the scene before him.

On top of the crimson sheets like three multicolored worms Dr. Fell, the blonde, and the black woman were locked in an obscene embrace, all struggling fiercely to achieve climax. At Longarm's appearance, Dr. Fell lifted his gleaming, bald head momentarily from between the thighs of the blonde, fixed Longarm with his malignant green eyes for an instant, then fell upon her once again, devouring hungrily.

Longarm felt as well as heard someone behind him.

He spun in time to see a huge bare-chested Chinaman bringing down a Turkish scimitar. The blade sliced through the air inches from Longarm's cheek as Longarm fired at the Chinaman. The echo of the gunshot seemed to go on forever, but the bullet appeared to have no effect at all as the bodyguard lifted his scimitar over his head a second time. Again Longarm fired, the blast reverberating like a cannon in the smoke-filled chamber. The Chinaman paused, dropped the scimitar, and sank to his knees, two bright black holes growing in his chest.

That was when Longarm saw Ti's bound body hanging to a post in the far corner of the room. Her head was drooped crookedly, and for a moment he thought she was dead.

He rushed over to her and slashed through the rawhide binding her wrists to the post. As she slumped into his arms, he swept her up and started from the room. By this time, however, the cloying, overpowering scent of opium was clouding his senses. He began to reel crazily. The forms on the bed shifted into unreal hallucinations, and he felt his breath coming in short, sharp bursts, as if he were racing up a hill.

Stumbling drunkenly, he stepped over the guard he had killed. As he did so, Dr. Fell stood upright on the bedspread, his long, hairless body gleaming with sweat, and held out to Longarm a long black opium pipe. As he did so, he lifted his head back and laughed—a long, mocking laugh that seemed to come from another time, another universe.

Longarm pushed himself through the doorway, kicked the door shut behind him, then carried Ti back to the passageway at the bottom of the stairwell. Propping her up against the stairs, Longarm turned on the kerosene barrel's spigot and let the kerosene pour out over the floor. Then, choosing one of the empty buckets, he filled it with kerosene, rushed back to the anteroom, and splashed it against the door. He went back for another bucket and emptied this one up and down the hallway leading to the bedroom.

Taking a couple of lanterns down from the wall, he returned to the bedroom. The hallway and the anteroom stank of kerosene. Pressing his ear against the door, he heard more laughter. Dr. Fell, it seemed, had no inkling yet of this night's attack on him and his corrupt empire. After that long, tedious coach ride from San Francisco, he had probably given orders not to be disturbed. He was anxious to sample the fresh opium and the two new girls he had brought back with him.

Stepping back out of the way, Longarm hurled the lantern at the door. As it erupted into flames, he ran back through the dungeon chamber and flung the second lamp at a river of kerosene rushing through the place. The entire dungeon went up with a sudden deep *whump*, the blast almost knocking Longarm to the floor. Once he reached the stairs, he swept Ti up into his arms and raced up the stairway. Emerging into the black-curtained corridor a moment later, he felt behind him a blast of heat like that from an open furnace, and quickly slammed the door shut behind him.

The ebony door with silver trim opened suddenly and Charlie Fiddle bolted through the doorway, Wan San right behind him. When Charlie saw Longarm and the limp burden he was carrying he pulled up, startled.

"Well, now!" he cried. "I was wondering where you'd got to. Is that Ti?"

Longarm nodded. "You've taken the house, have you?"

Charlie's eyes were alight with the success of the attack. "Taken it and then some! I'd say there's maybe fifteen to twenty dead Chinamen dressed in black and silver littering the slopes leading up here and half that number dead in the house behind me, most of them with crossbow bolts stickin' out of their chests."

"How many people did we lose?"

"Hardly any, I'd say. Maybe three, four."

"Good."

Charlie had reached Longarm by then. Peering at Ti, he frowned in sudden anger. "Mother of God," he whispered. "The poor child."

"She's alive. That's something," Longarm said. "Now let's get the hell out of here."

"But, Longarm, I ain't found Fell yet!"

"Never mind, Charlie. I found him."

Burt appeared behind them in the doorway, Sanchez on his heels. "This place is going up!" Burt cried. "We better get the hell out of here!"

The black smoke pouring up through the floor halted all further discussion.

Halfway down the slope a few moments later, Longarm and the others paused to look back up through the pines. The night had been turned into day by the fierce, leaping flames that now engulfed Dr. Fell's mansion. Standing there with Ti still in his arms, Longarm thought he could hear again the mindless laughter of those two women coiled on the bed with Fell.

Longarm turned back around and led the plunge down the slope.

Chapter 11

The next day the inhabitants of Celestial City celebrated their victory over the tyrannical Dr. Fell with an impromptu holiday. Long, twisting paper dragons danced in the street to the accompaniment of constant bursts of firecrackers. A pleased Ti-Ling and her father watched from an open window above the tailor shop, the joy of Ti-Ling's release blooming through the horror of her brief imprisonment and the cruel bruises she had sustained.

The festivities lasted until late in the afternoon. That was when the sentries Charlie had posted on the other side of the marsh reported sighting a considerable body of gunslicks moving through the pass on their way to Celestial City. It was estimated that the force would not reach the marsh until well after dark, and it was said to number at least fifty hard-bitten gunslicks.

They were led by Malcolm Hartridge and were bringing with them at least five ore wagons for transporting back with them to the silver mines the Celestials they were expecting to capture. Hartridge had no way of knowing that Dr. Fell was no longer a factor in his schemes, which only meant Hartridge would attack as ruthlessly as ever.

Longarm convened a second war council in the town's saloon. The council was made up of Longarm, Charlie, Burt, and Ling Chan, who—despite his advanced years—had brought down two of Dr. Fell's men on the pine slopes while suffering a mild flesh wound himself. Stepping first through the batwings, Longarm found the gleaming, immaculate saloon again nearly deserted. There were only three patrons. Behind him came Ling Chan. One nod from this ancient personage and the barkeep vanished, the three patrons vacating the place as swiftly and silently as he.

Longarm and Charlie moved a couple of tables together and spread out over them a rough map of the valley showing clearly the marsh, the road leading across it, and Celestial City. After a short discussion it was agreed to allow the advance elements of the Celestial force to strike at Hartridge's men only after they began moving across the marsh. At that point they would be unable to turn back and would be forced to continue on to the bridge, where the main body of skirmishers would be posted.

Once Hartridge's men broke through—as everyone agreed they probably would—Hartridge would find the entire town an aroused hornet's nest, a trap from which this time they would be unable to escape.

Charlie had already sent a sizeable force across the marsh and was planning to join them just before sundown. Burt and Sanchez would command the bowmen at the bridge, with Longarm organizing and leading the townsmen's citizens when finally they joined the fray.

The disposition of their forces thus settled, Charlie leaned back and asked if anyone had questions. Longarm promptly asked if his bowmen needed more bolts.

"Wan San assures me his small factory will have at least a hundred bolts ready by sundown," Charlie replied. "I'll distribute them when I move out."

"You think that'll be enough?"

"Most of the bowmen I got stationed over there already have four bolts apiece. That was enough last night. More than enough."

"Why they still usin' them crossbows?" Sanchez wanted to know. "We captured enough guns and ammunition last night to outfit a small army."

"My guess is these here slants feel more comfortable with their crossbows," Burt said. "Ain't that right, Ling Chan?"

Ling Chan smiled and bowed his head. "It is as you say," the old Chinaman replied, his soft, polite voice heavy with respect for the man who had just referred to his people as slants. "Wan San's bolts are silent and kill with great efficiency. It is good the Indians do not have such weapons."

"What the Apaches got is near as good," said Sanchez. "Them little black arrows they shoot can be just as deadly—and just as quiet."

"It's a good point, though," Longarm said. "It wouldn't hurt any if we were to back up the Celestials with our own firepower. But let them take out as many of Hartridge's men as they can with their crossbows before we move in on them."

Charlie chuckled, took out a long clay pipe Ling Chan had given him, and began tamping in fresh tobacco. "Them silent bolts do a good job, all right. Yes, sir, they hit like a fist out of nowhere, and knock a feller clear into the next world before he knows he's in a battle."

That point settled, Longarm looked over at Ling Chan and told him it would be all right for the barkeep to return now to his saloon. The war council could maybe use a few drinks before they set out to fight their second war in as many days.

Charlie Fiddle had chosen his best bowman to serve as his lieutenant. His name was Tin Sein. Charlie called him Tin. He spoke passable English and was a slim, small-boned fellow with alert eyes. What impressed Charlie the most was that he never had to tell Tin anything more than once. Like the rest of his platoon, Tin was armed with a crossbow and six bolts. As Charlie had seen when they were invading Dr. Fell's mining operation, Tin's accuracy was astonishing and deadly. Tin Sein called Charlie "General," and Charlie saw no need to dispute his lieutenant on the matter. They had twelve men with them, half loaders, the others good crossbowmen whose lethal accuracy had already been proven.

They were waiting in the marsh for Hartridge's small army to reach them, crouched down in rushes on both sides of the roadway, at a spot where it was most narrow. Charlie's plan was a bit tricky, but it was ingenious, and Tin liked it and had little difficulty explaining it to their men.

Under cover of darkness, half of Charlie's force would climb into one of the ore wagons and wait until Hartridge's men were at least three-quarters of the way across the marsh before opening up on the unsuspecting riders escorting the wagons. As soon as this engagement began, the remainder of Charlie's force, led by Tin, would attack from the rear, driving Hartridge and his men forward toward the bridge.

"Look," whispered Tin, pointing.

Charlie nodded. The sentries had all been pulled back and for the past fifteen minutes or so, the rumble of the approaching wagons and the chink of bits had been getting steadily louder. Now they could see the vanguard of Hartridge's force moving out onto the roadway. Charlie and his men lowered themselves still deeper into the icy water.

Before long Hartridge's gunmen were passing within a few feet of them, the sound of their low, rough laughter filling the night with menace.

Charlie glanced up at the sky. There was no moon, and for that he was grateful, but the starlight was so bright this high up, it was almost as bright as moonlight.

Charlie tapped Tin lightly on the shoulder and moved closer to the roadway, his six men moving with him. A rider's horse kicked up a mud clod, which struck Charlie on the shoulder. He paid it no heed as the riders kept on past his position. Already he had counted close to thirty-five riders, and from the look of it, their earlier estimate of fifty men was not far off.

The wagons, lumbering and wallowing in the soft soil, loomed suddenly against the night sky. Charlie had chosen his spot well. So narrow was the roadway here that none of Hartridge's gunslicks were riding alongside the wagons. Charlie waited for the team of horses to plod by, then gained the road. Racing to keep up with the wagon, he boosted himself over the side. Safely in the wagon, he extended his hand to the bowman behind him, and in less than a few seconds all six men were crouched down safely inside the wagon.

They kept down until Charlie judged they had reached the spot where the action should begin, beyond the point of no return for Hartridge and his gunmen. Charlie nodded to his men. The three bowmen clambered up the front of the ore wagon and steadied their crossbows.

Colt in hand, Charlie climbed up beside them and saw the bridge materializing out of the night ahead of them. They were getting pretty damned close to it, he realized. He nodded quickly to his bowmen.

Aiming at the nearest riders, they released their bolts, passed their crossbows down to their loaders, lifted their second crossbows, and sent three more bolts—the only sound through all this the sudden whip forward of the bowstring and a kind of soft whirring as the bolts seared through the air. The driver of the horses pulling their ore wagon was the first to go, slumping lifelessly in his seat, causing the team to slow down some but not halt. Three, then four riders slid or toppled from their horses. A fifth rider simply collapsed forward over the neck of his mount.

There was immediate pandemonium. Gunfire erupted from the invaders' ranks as they shot blindly into the night while trying to wheel their horses on the narrow trail. The men only succeeded in getting in each other's way, probably wounding each other in their wild panic. Meanwhile, Charlie's bowmen continued to rain their lethal shower of death upon the milling riders, the eerie silence and terrible effectiveness of the crossbows enough to unhinge even the most cold-blooded of Hartridge's men.

Turning around, Charlie saw the drivers of the other ore wagons pull up hastily and reach for their guns. Charlie jumped down into the bed of the ore wagon, raced back, then boosted himself up over the tailgate and began firing at the other teamsters. As the nearest driver toppled from his seat, Charlie glanced up and saw the riders behind the ore wagons suddenly begin to wheel and fire blindly into the night around them, which meant Tin's force had sprung into action at their rear, effectively bottling them up between themselves and the stalled wagons. These ten or twenty of Hartridge's riders were now effectively cut off from the main body.

Glancing back over his shoulder, Charlie saw Hartridge's forces still milling frantically about in an effort to get a bead on their attackers. Gunfire and the doomed cries of terrified men pitching from their horses filled the night. It looked as if things were going nicely at this end. Charlie dropped to the ground to run back and give Tin a hand. As he ran between the last two wagons, a crouching teamster lifted his Greener and blasted Charlie with both barrels.

Charlie never knew what hit him as the double-O buckshot flung him out over the dark waters.

Sanchez and Burt both saw Hartridge at the same time. Leading his men with surprising vigor, Hartridge was shooting down at the coolies and shouting to his men to forget the wagons and charge the bridge.

"Here they come!" Sanchez called across the bridge to Burt.

Sanchez was on the left side of the bridge, Burt on the right. They had stationed their men both under the bridge and up on the walkway. Now, bolts fitted to their crossbows, they watched Hartridge and at least twenty of his men break away from the melee around the wagons and gallop toward them, Hartridge in the lead.

Aware that they were charging through an ambush, the gunslicks fired indiscriminately about them as they rode, counting on their firepower and speed to get them through. Sanchez aimed his Colt at Hartridge and waited. He had told his men not to loose their bolts until he had fired. Burt and his men were waiting also.

Hartridge loomed. He had a pearl-handled sixgun and was punching the night with lead as he rode. Sanchez tracked him carefully and fired. But the moment he did, Hartridge ducked his head as he turned his horse directly for the center of the bridge. Sanchez missed, but that did not matter. The air was suddenly alive with the thrumming of bowstrings. At least five men screamed and went backward off their mounts.

Still Hartridge and his remaining riders swept up onto the bridge. The sound of their horses' hoofs filled the night with thunder. The coolies were sending the bolts after them, but the riders were staying low and moving fast. Then Sanchez saw Burt standing on the bridge railing. He suddenly hurled himself at one of the last riders, dragging him from his horse.

As Hartridge and his men crossed the bridge and clattered toward Celestial City, Sanchez saw Burt still on the bridge, struggling with the rider he had pulled from his horse. Unsheathing his knife, Sanchez jumped over the railing and raced across the bridge to help Burt. Before he could reach them, a muffled shot sounded. Sanchez saw the gunman push back and get slowly to his feet, the Colt in his hand still smoking. Before him on the ground, Burt was twisting slowly in agony, his hands trying to hold in his gut.

The gunslick heard Sanchez coming. He spun and got off a quick shot, but Sanchez ducked under it, left his feet, and slammed into the man's mid-section. He folded under the impetus of Sanchez's charge and went down under the Mexican. He clubbed up at Sanchez desperately, a big man with wild eyes and a handlebar mustache. Sanchez brought his knife up, then down, burying it to the hilt in the man's chest. Pulling the blade free, Sanchez leaned forward and sliced the man's neck from ear to ear. As the head lolled back, Sanchez hurried over to Burt's side.

Burt looked up at him with wild, agonized eyes. "Jesus, Sanchez, I'm gutshot!"

"You'll be all right."

"No, I won't! My guts are spilling out. I can't even hold them in."

Sanchez looked and saw that Burt was right. He had never seen a man recover from such a wound as this. He felt sick himself at the sight of it. "You'll be all right," he repeated to Burt bleakly.

"Kill me, Sanchez," Burt pleaded. "Do it quick. I don't want to go this way."

"You talk crazy."

"I'd do it for you, Sanchez. You know I would."

Sanchez stood up and looked down at his dying friend.

Yes, he realized, Burt would have done it for him if he had asked. He had become that good a friend over these past weeks. Sanchez took out his Colt, turned around, and angrily waved back the coolies now crowding around.

Then he turned back to his friend, aimed carefully, and fired.

Counting the riders still remaining with Hartridge, Longarm was pleased. There were less than twenty men left of an original force that was supposed to have numbered at least fifty. He was standing at the head of an alley, his hand up over his shoulder, waiting.

Longarm saw Hartridge gallop past, his men strung out behind him. It was obvious Hartridge was hoping to make it through the town safely, then hole up with Dr. Fell. Longarm dropped his arm and raced out into the street, his sixgun blazing.

Behind him came his militia, loosing their deadly bolts at the riders. The toll was enormous. The first volley smashed at least five riders from their horses. As the rest of Longarm's militia swarmed out of storefronts and alleys ahead of Hartridge's force, sending wave after wave of their deadly bolts into the horsemen's midst, Hartridge realized he was now effectively cut off. Wheeling his horse, he headed for an alley across the street from Longarm and galloped into it.

On foot, Longarm raced through the milling formation of riders and into the alley after Hartridge. Horse and rider were visible just ahead of him. Before Hartridge could turn down the back alley, Longarm held up and fired. The horse went down quickly, as if its legs had been severed by the shot. Racing after Hartridge, he saw the man regain his feet and duck down the back alley.

Taking after him, Longarm had little difficulty gaining on his stocky figure. When he judged himself close enough, he held up and fired. Unhit, Hartridge ducked out of sight. Longarm slowed, wary of an ambush. Suddenly he heard a cry—one of sheer, unadulterated terror.

Longarm raced toward the sound, cut down a narrow alley, and pulled up in astonishment. Hartridge was on the ground, struggling fearfully, his eyes wide in terror. Sitting on his chest was the tailor, Chou Li-Fan. In one hand Li-Fan held a pair of scissors, the points of which were already drawing blood as they sliced into Hartridge's neck. In Chou Li-Fan's other hand was a hatchet. He was holding it high over his head.

Before Longarm could stop him, the tailor brought the hatchet down, splitting cleanly Hartridge's forehead.

Two days later, it was a sadder, wiser group that trooped into Celestial City's saloon for their last war council.

Ling Chan was among those in attendance, as were Tai Wong and Wan San. These two were now members by virtue of their remarkable success in arming Celestial City's militia. Tin Sein was also a member. When Sanchez and Longarm had moved out with a small force to clear the ore wagons from the road, they found a silent, murderous battle on the other side of the stalled wagons, with Tin Sein and two other Chinese holding off seven well-armed men.

The barkeep pushed together a few tables and the council members sat down around it. Longarm and Sanchez ordered whiskey. The Chinese were content to puff on their clay pipes. It was a solemn occasion. They had just come from a tree-shaded hill above Celestial City where they had finished burying their dead. Charlie and Burt had been buried side by side on a slope that gave a fine view of the valley and mountains beyond. Longarm had tried to find words, but he had given it up as a bad job. But Sanchez, his head bowed over the graves, had said a prayer in Spanish.

The barkeep placed a bottle and two glasses in front of

Longarm and Sanchez. Longarm poured for both of them, then looked across the table at Ling Chan.

"What now, Ling?"

"We leave this hateful valley."

"It need not be hateful any longer. You got a nice place here."

"Many years ago, we build this village—away from our enemies. We hope maybe we grow rice here and send for our wives. We had yet much gold from our days in the mines, but soon that was gone. Then comes here to this valley Dr. Fell. It has been bad for us, this place. It is not our land. Now that we no longer must submit to a tyrant, we will go home." Ling Chan smiled then, his old face growing almost youthful. "We will sail in past the Dragon's Eye and into the Tiger's Mouth," he said softly, "and from there we will be able to see the rice fields on the eastern shore and the Pagoda of Nine Stories . . ."

He held up suddenly, aware that he had been digressing.

"I beg your pardon," he said to Longarm and Sanchez. "You must forgive the ramblings of an old man. It has been too many years since I have seen the land of our ancestors."

"How you goin' to get there, Ling?" Sanchez asked.

"We will buy passage on the fabled liners of this rich country. We will return to our wives as we promised to do when we left—as rich men."

"Rich?" Sanchez repeated. "But there's no gold here."

"There's the jade," Longarm reminded Sanchez.

"Yes," agreed Ling, addressing Longarm. "We will use these wagons provided by Hartridge. And the few survivors of his force will learn what it is like to work for another without payment." Ling smiled confidently. "There is much jade left in the mine, and we will find more in the slopes and valleys before we depart. In San Francisco we will see to those who dealt with Dr. Fell. Then we shall return to our land, the lovely Pearl River delta."

"I hope it works out for you."

"It will, Longarm," spoke up Tin Sein. "Charlie Fiddle trained our warriors well. They will see to it that we return safely to the land of our ancestors."

"You mean there's a chance you'll be using those fearsome crossbows in San Francisco?"

"If we are forced to. But does it matter where we use these silent messengers, as long as our cause is just?"

Longarm frowned. He knew about Tong wars and what they could do to a Chinese enclave, but he also knew how cruelly Dr. Fell had used his own people here in Celestial City. And, besides, when people started talking about what was just and unjust, he usually dealt himself out.

"I guess not," he agreed.

"You are both welcome to stay here as our guests, if you wish," Ling Chan told them. "It will be weeks before we are ready to leave."

"Thanks, but I'll be pulling out tomorrow morning," Longarm said.

"Not me," said Sanchez. "If you do not mind, Señor Ling, I'd just as soon accompany your people to San Francisco. I figure nobody will be lookin' for this hombre in a wagon train full of orientals."

"That is true," admitted Ling. "It would be an excellent way for a hunted man to travel undetected."

"Yes," said Sanchez nervously, picking up his glass. "That is what I think, too."

The next morning Sanchez rode with Longarm as far as the pines on the other side of the marshland. By that time, the sun was just poking up over the mountains rimming the valley. Longarm pulled his chestnut to a halt and reached across his saddlehorn to shake the Mexican's hand.

"You sure you won't change your mind?" Longarm asked. "I know Billy Vail would speak up for you before the judge.

You were one of my deputies, don't forget."

"Maybe this Billy Vail, he do what you say. I do not think you lie to me, Longarm. But it will take more, much more than him to save me from the hangman's rope."

"I never asked, Sanchez. And you don't have to tell me if you don't want to. What'd you do?"

"I killed a man."

"A robbery?"

"A matter of honor, *amigo*. Over a woman. I would never kill a man during a robbery. That would be insane." He shrugged. "But this girl, she was spitfire. I love her still. She was worth it."

"Murder is a tough rap to beat."

"So you see. This Mexican, he have no choice. Before long he will be in California—and from there, who knows—maybe even China." His teeth flashed. "I tell you what, Longarm. These Chinese girls I like. Especially that one you take to bed."

"Ti-Ling?"

He nodded.

"Give Ti-Ling my best, will you? She was unhappy she could not ride out with me this morning. Her father did not approve."

"I will give her your best, *amigo*. Maybe I will give her my best, too."

Longarm laughed. "I can see why you get into quarrels over women, Sanchez. Goodbye and good luck."

"God go with you, *amigo!*"

Sanchez wheeled his horse and loped down the slope. Longarm watched him, a smile on his face. Reaching the flat, Sanchez took off his sombrero and waved. Longarm waved back.

Turning the chestnut, Longarm soon reached the pines. He was still smiling, remembering the night before, which he had spent with Ti-Ling. It had been a feverish, exhausting night—their last night together—and at its close, before Longarm had dropped off finally to sleep, Ti-Ling had kept him awake long enough to ask about someone, her almond-shaped eyes glowing as she did.

She had asked about Sanchez.

Chapter 12

Longarm pulled off the road and looked down once again upon Green's Creek. A horse stood swaybacked and sleepy before the hotel, store owners were sweeping off the wooden boardwalks, and the hostler sat on a barrel in front of the livery, whittling. The town was coming awake—and Longarm was already beginning to wince at the steady, fateful pounding of the stamping mill, its tyrannical beat still echoing off the surrounding mountains.

He kneed his chestnut back onto the road and kept on toward the town. Clopping onto the main street about an hour later, he dismounted in front of a small restaurant, hankering after some apple pie, if there was any left, and a steaming cup of coffee. It had been a long, wearisome ride. The jolly, rosy-cheeked woman behind the counter had a dimple in her chin. She smiled when she saw Longarm approach the counter and actually seemed to mean it.

He ordered pie and coffee and was delighted to find that such was indeed possible, even at this hour. He didn't like sitting at the counter, so when his order came, he took it with him over to an empty table near the window. There he ate his pie and drank his coffee slowly while he studied the town, now fully awake.

Longarm was not enjoying this lonely ride back to Denver—and Billy Vail—without the man he had been assigned to bring back, and Green's Creek reminded him of just how close he had come to apprehending Tomlinson. It also reminded him of one very beautiful Dragon Lady. Lotus Wong had enabled him to escape Hartridge's mine, and for that he was grateful. The trouble was, he had a nagging feeling things had not turned out the way she had expected—or wanted.

His survival of that breakout seemed not to have pleased her at all.

Of course, it was only a feeling, but coupled with her honest statement that no man was her friend, that she used them just as they used her, he had found himself turning over and over in his mind her role in that escape. As for her claim she had sent Abe Goshen to warn him, though he did not find it far-fetched, it sure did stretch things a bit. He had believed it at the time because it was something he wanted very much to believe.

Now, with him on his way back to Denver empty-handed, he had the unmistakable feeling that he had been taken, that Lotus Wong was up there in that hotel of hers, laughing at him. Perhaps he had better forget about riding on through. Maybe now was as good a time as any to see if she really could outlast him.

Longarm finished his coffee, dropped a coin on the table, and left the restaurant.

• • •

After seeing to his mount, he registered at the hotel, visited the barber shop, then made a few purchases, after which he entered the Miners' Palace. He spent the rest of that morning and afternoon at a small table at the rear of the saloon.

As before, the barkeep had no Maryland rye, so Longarm made do with whiskey instead. He made no effort to hide himself from the patrons, and news of his presence spread rapidly, causing a noticeable increase in the flow of traffic through the batwings. Not a single man who entered the place failed to glance at least once in Longarm's direction.

He was still remembered, it seemed, as the man who had outgunned three gunslicks, killing one and wounding another. That he was back in Green's Creek aroused in the townsmen the hope of yet another, equally exciting gun battle. Longarm, meanwhile, said nothing as he kept on sipping his whiskey. And waited.

It was dark when Lotus sent for him. One of her housemaids squeezed through the noisy crush of patrons and delivered her note. It was short and to the point:

My dear Custis,

When can I expect you? It has been so long. I am absolutely positive I can outlast you this time after all that whiskey you've been consuming.

Lotus.

Longarm thanked the girl and finished the bottle. Then he stood up, carefully positioned on his head the black Stetson he had procured in Celestial City, and left the saloon.

As he walked down the street toward the hotel, he patted his vest to make sure the derringer was resting in its accustomed place. That morning he had purchased rounds for the derringer and reloaded his Colt with fresh cartridges. He had lost his .44 to Pincherman, but the cross-draw rig he had not taken, and it was still in good condition. Longarm comforted himself with the knowledge he would be able to get himself another double-action when he returned to Denver. He would most likely have to file off the sight and get accustomed to a new weapon's action, but that would not be too difficult.

He reached the hotel and went up to his room. He had kicked his boots off and was reclining on his bed, his Colt under his pillow and his vest folded carefully over the headboard behind him, when a soft knock came on the door.

"Custis?"

"Come on in," he called. "The door's unlocked."

The door opened. Lotus slipped in and turned to him. "Well?"

Longarm was astonished. She was still as beautiful as ever, perhaps even more so, for this time she had managed to banish completely any trace of her Yankee heritage. Now she was all Chinese, every sinuous curve, from her high cheekbones all the way down to her exquisite ankles. She was wearing a black silk dress with wide sleeves decorated by a single gold trim that ran down one side. It was buttoned high on the neck, swept past her ample hips, and reached all the way to her instep, the slit in the skirt trimmed in gold and reaching as high as her knee.

She closed the door and turned to him. "Well?"

"You have changed, Lotus."

"No. I have become what I always was, Custis. A princess of China."

He smiled and sat up. "Well, now. Are you sure you still want to dally with a commoner like me—a plain, ordinary saddle tramp with a badge?"

"You are some saddle tramp, Custis," she told him, gliding toward him. "And I am more woman than you have ever known. Tonight I will prove it."

"That so?"

"But not here. Not in this bleak hotel room."

"Where, then?"

"Follow me."

He slipped on his vest and coat, then reached under the pillow for his gun.

"No, Custis," she told him. "You will not need that."

"I'd feel pretty naked without my shooting iron."

"I said no." She took a small pearl-handled derringer from one of her sleeves and cocked it with her thumb.

Longarm sighed. "Well, now, when you put it like that."

"Follow me."

From the outside, Lotus's hotel, though it was the largest structure in Green's Creek, did not look a bit unusual. It was just a large, square, undistinguished building four stories high. But as Lotus led him through doors and down long, dimly lit hallways, and then finally up a thickly carpeted stairway, he realized there was considerably more to Lotus Wong's hostelry than anyone in Green's Creek imagined.

And considerably more to Lotus Wong, as well.

She pushed through the final door, which swung open immediately at her light touch. Turning, she smiled and beckoned him in with a graceful sweep of her hand—the one holding the derringer.

Longarm found himself in a bedchamber that had to have been conceived by someone puffing on an opium pipe. There was a huge bed in the center, high enough for steps leading up to it. Great ebony chairs stood in the four corners, looking more like thrones than chairs. A huge fireplace, big enough for five men to walk into it abreast, covered one entire wall. It was constructed of a black stone, most likely basalt.

The only colors in the room were red and black. In all

four corners, over the thronelike chairs, red lamps glowed, filling the room with a lurid luminescence. The massive silken drapes that covered the walls were blacker than midnight, and were covered with the usual Chinese dragons and mountain scenes, all rendered in intricately woven red thread, made of silk, he had no doubt.

As he moved closer to the bed, he glanced up and saw that the ceiling over it was covered with drapes as well, and these drapes also displayed images traced in red silk, but these were not images of nature or of dragons. They were the entwined, convoluted images of naked men and women, copulating frantically in as many different positions as the human physique made possible.

It was a masterpiece of erotica, and as Lotus reached the bed just ahead of him and whirled about to face Longarm, she shed her black silk dress in one quick movement and stood before him naked, her olive figure shimmering in the lamps' livid light.

But she still held the ivory-handled derringer.

"You going to shoot me or screw me to death?" Longarm asked her.

"I don't know which for now. Perhaps you can make that decision yourself. Come here."

He did as she bid and let her long, swift fingers undress him. He managed to take off his coat and vest himself, while she busied herself with his pants. He threw his coat, vest, and shirt down on the floor beside the bed and stepped out of his pants and underdrawers. With a pleased sigh at sight of him, she drew him onto the black silken coverlet of the immense bed.

"Get rid of the derringer," he told her.

"Of course." She pushed it under a pillow and wrapped her arms about him eagerly, planting her lips on his. They worked furiously, devouring him.

Longarm was wary. But he was also a man. And this

was a woman in heat. She was like a natural force, and he felt as capable of stemming it as he would of turning aside a cataract or damning a rapids in springtime. All he could do was allow her fierce, unholy passion to sweep him along with her—and before long, that was exactly what happened.

First he was on top, and then it was her turn. He came and then she did, but still she remained unsatisfied. She astonished him with her ingenuity in keeping him erect. But it was more than ingenuity, it was the hot, pulsing insatiability of her passion that swept him along.

At last, pounding to a climax atop her one more time, he looked down and saw her straining face, the dark penumbra of her hair whipping out over her pillow as she flung her head from side to side, and knew this was going to have to be it. If she wanted more, she would simply have to bring in reinforcements. She had outlasted him.

Sagging at last to the bedspread beside her, he draped an arm over her shoulder and felt her silken skin quiver excitedly.

"Now I want you to go in the rear," she told him. "It will be so much tighter for you. You will see. It will bring you to life!"

Longarm groaned softly. "No more, Lotus. You win. You've outlasted me. Congratulations."

She sat up quickly, her face livid with rage.

"You do as I say!" she screamed. "I am not finished yet. I have just begun. You are no man if you cannot satisfy me!"

"No man could satisfy you, Lotus."

From behind him Longarm heard a voice. "That is not entirely true, Longarm."

Longarm spun about. A tall, imperious figure was approaching the foot of the bed. Dr. Fell! The design and color of his dress were similar to Lotus's gown, except of course that he was wearing trousers. In short, his attire was a perfect match for Lotus's, and had obviously been fashioned by the same hands.

Dr. Fell's great dome of a forehead dominated his face, which was etched into satanic overtones by his mustache and beard. Above his high cheekbones, his eyes were emerald fires glowing in the sockets of his long, ascetic face. In that opium-fogged bedchamber beneath his mansion, Dr. Fell had resembled some kind of lizard or serpent, an alien creature cavorting with other alien creatures. Now, as he advanced on Longarm and smiled, he looked more human, perhaps, but still a powerful incarnation of evil, a figure from another world.

As indeed he was.

"Are you surprised to see me alive, Longarm?"

"Yes."

"You will be happy to know that my two playmates on that occasion are also still healthy." He walked over to one of the chairs and sat down in it, his emerald eyes regarding Longarm with the same unblinking attention as a reptile half out of water.

Longarm began pulling on his longjohns. He felt at a disadvantage standing naked before such a grim and compelling personage.

"Are you going somewhere?" Dr. Fell asked, smiling.

"Back to Denver," Longarm replied, reaching for his pants.

"You really think so?"

Longarm continued to dress. Reaching down for his shirt, he slipped it on. "Why not? The man I came for has escaped. There's no sense in wasting my time looking for him in these hills."

With a sudden, inexplicable cry of rage, Lotus flung herself upon him, bearing him to the floor while she beat and clawed at him about his head and shoulders. Longarm was grateful she had forgotten in the heat of her fury the derringer she had leveled on him earlier.

Dr. Fell strode from his chair and flung Lotus off Longarm's back. His strength was enormous. She was airborne for a moment before landing on the bed. With a squeal of rage, she reached in under the pillow for her derringer. Longarm had expected that. Leaping on her, he slapped the gun from her hand and sent it skittering into a corner, where it lay like something alive, its pearl handle glowing redly.

"Enough, Lotus!" Dr. Fell cried.

At once Lotus pulled in upon herself and bottled her fury while still watching Longarm malevolently, her eyes flashing pure hatred.

"Why, Lotus?" Longarm asked, reaching down for his vest. "What the hell's got into you?"

Lotus refused to reply. She suddenly glanced fearfully at Dr. Fell, who turned and strode back to his chair. Slumping into it, he let his emerald eyes rest on Lotus. They were as cold as death.

"It seems," Dr. Fell told Longarm, his resonant voice filling the black room, "that for some time my bride-to-be has cultivated an inordinate passion for one of your race. I learned of this only today."

Lotus's face went white. She sat up in the bed and moved back until her shoulders were resting against the headboard.

Longarm should have been surprised, but he wasn't. Deep inside, he had known something like this all along. The man Dr. Fell was referring to was Jed Tomlinson. It all came together—Lotus sending him to that ghost town where Tomlinson was waiting for him, then her bribing the guards at the mine so he would break out and die in the attempt. He remembered how disturbed she had been to learn that he had even survived Pincherman and his crony.

"You mean Jed Tomlinson," Longarm said.

"Yes," Dr. Fell replied. "I am afraid so."

Longarm turned quickly to her. "Where's Tomlinson?"

"Dead!" she spat. "When I got back from the mine, Jed was waiting for me, bleeding to death from wounds you inflicted! He died before I could save him."

"And since then she has been inconsolable, Longarm," explained Dr. Fell, leaning his massive dome back against this chair. "I had no idea why she acted as she did. She told me only that she wished to humiliate you, then kill you. She did not tell me why. Now I know."

Longarm was fully dressed now. His Colt was back in his room, but his derringer was sitting in his watch-fob pocket, fully loaded. Neither Lotus nor Dr. Fell was armed, though both had to be fully aware of that pearl-handled derringer glowing softly in the corner.

Longarm started for the door—and saw there was no door.

Dr. Fell chuckled; the sound of it was deep and deadly as it filled the room. "You are not going anywhere, Marshal, not after the trouble you have caused me—and could still cause if I were to be so foolish as to let you walk out of here. I am sure you understand."

Longarm did. He was in a bottle and Dr. Fell had just corked it. As he saw it, his only hope was to muddy the waters some. "You going to kill me and let Lotus go free? You think you can ever trust her again?"

Dr. Fell regarded Lotus coldly, a concentration in his eyes so terrible it was almost painful to witness. Lotus stirred fearfully on the bed. Like Longarm, she was waiting for his answer.

"Perhaps I will."

"But you are not sure. You know you can't trust her."

"Yes, Marshal." He sighed wearily. "I suppose it does mean that."

He got up from the chair and walked over toward the bed. As he did so, he took from his sleeve a long silver dagger. Lotus flung up her arm.

"No!" she cried.

"Yes," said Dr. Fell. "The marshal has put his finger on it. I can never trust you. Never again."

Flinging herself off the bed, she leaped for the corner and swept up her derringer. Dr. Fell was upon her almost as quickly. His dagger lifted, then fell with a terrible swiftness. At almost the same time, there was a muffled shot, and then another. Longarm saw Dr. Fell straighten, stagger, then turn and walk back to his chair. He made it just barely and slumped into it with a soft, bitter sigh of pain.

Ignoring him, Longarm hurried over to Lotus. She had been cut cruelly by Dr. Fell's knife, in the back and in the chest. She was not dead, but as she gazed up at him, she was able to generate malice so strong it sickened him. He pulled back.

A door behind the drapes at the far end of the room was flung open. The drapes parted and two enormous Chinamen appeared, each carrying a long, scimitar-like blade. They were dressed in black like their master, and their heads were clean-shaven, except for a topknot bound with a red ribbon.

Dr. Fell stirred himself and waved his arm at Longarm. "Kill him," he rasped. *"Kill him!"*

Longarm reached into his vest pocket and palmed his derringer. As the two guards saw this, they pulled up, but only for a moment.

"I'm warning you," said Longarm. "Keep back or I'll fire."

Still the two came on. Longarm fired twice, carefully. His first round caught the nearest one in the chest, knocking him back; his second round caught the other one in the face, turning one side of it to mush. Both men kept going for a moment or two, then toppled clumsily to the floor.

Stepping quickly around them, Longarm clawed through the drapes until he found the doorknob. He turned it and was stepping through the door when two powerful hands closed like a steel vise about his neck and flung him around.

It was Dr. Fell, his face a satanic mask of fury as his hands tightened about Longarm's neck.

Longarm struggled to pull free, but the more he struggled the more tightly the man's hands closed about his windpipe as he dragged Longarm back into the room. Longarm's senses began to reel. He thought he heard someone coming up behind him. In that instant, Dr. fell paused momentarily and Longarm made one last effort to break free. Shifting his feet and using both hands, he managed to fling the doctor around.

That was when he saw Lotus bring the knife down. Dr. Fell uttered a soft moan as he was pulled back momentarily; then slowly he relaxed his grip on Longarm's neck. Clawing free from Dr. Fell's grip, Longarm stepped back, struggling to breathe. For a few terrible moments, his breath came only in sharp, painful gasps.

As Dr. Fell sagged to the floor, Lotus stepped back in horror, the knife falling from her hand. Then she dropped to Dr. Fell's side, looking up in despair at Longarm as she did so.

"It was you I wanted to kill," she sobbed weakly. "You! Not him!"

Then she toppled forward lifelessly onto Dr. Fell's body.

Sitting at a table in the bar at the Windsor Hotel, Denver's largest and finest, Longarm poured Billy Vail another drink. Marshal Billy Vail needed it if he was to believe the tale Longarm was telling him.

". . . So let me get this straight," Billy Vail was saying. "This here big Chinaman with the bald head—the one you call Dr. Fell—he almost strangled you even though he had two bullets in him?"

"Right, chief. And it took Lotus to bring him down with a knife in the back."

"I'd call that poetic justice, wouldn't you?"

Longarm tossed down another shot of Maryland rye, then peeled the wrapping off a fresh cheroot. "I suppose."

"But just between you and me, Longarm, I would feel a whole lot better if you'd seen Jed Tomlinson's body—or, better yet, brought it back with you."

"Take my word for it. He's dead."

"You sure of that?"

"I hit him that night twice. And then I never saw hide nor hair of him again. And besides, Lotus was a very unhappy woman. The only way I can explain her fury was the fact of his death."

Billy Vail wiped his beefy face with his hand, then blinked down into his empty shot glass. "I suppose that makes sense. Only thing I can't figure is how a woman in her right mind would prefer Tomlinson to one of my deputy marshals. Just don't make any kind of sense."

He grinned boozily at Longarm and refilled their glasses.

"I don't mind telling you, Longarm, I was beginning to worry. So was Wallace. We figured you'd bought it this time. Wallace wanted to go after you, but I told him there was no need to panic."

"You were right."

"Another week, though, and I'd'a gone lookin' myself."

Despite himself, Longarm was moved by the old chief's concern.

"Oh, there's just one more thing," Vail said, pulling a dodger out of his back pocket and smoothing it out on the table. "This here jasper's Miguel Sanchez. Now you mentioned this afternoon them fellers you was with in that mine—an old prospector and two others. One of them you said was a Mexican. That right?"

"Yeah. That's right."

"Is this him?"

Longarm pulled the dodger closer and looked over the

crude drawing. It did a pretty good job of capturing Sanchez's expression and manner, though it made him look a little more wild and desperate than Longarm knew him to be. Sanchez was wanted for a killing, all right—and it did have something to do with a woman, that and a wedding that never took place.

Longarm looked up from the dodger. "Could be, but I wouldn't want to swear on it. This sure isn't a very good likeness. Give me a couple of days to think on it."

"I'd give you a year and you wouldn't swear on it. Here, let me have that."

Longarm handed the dodger back to Vail.

Taking it from Longarm, Vail tore it in half, then waved over the bartender. Handing the torn dodger to the man, he said, "Throw this away for me, will you, Sam—and bring another bottle for me and my friend. He just eloped from the backside of hell, and I'm purely glad to see him!"

Leaning back in his chair, Longarm mused on what Billy Vail had just said. In a way, the old lawman was not far from the truth. In those distant hills deep in the Rockies, he had come across strange worlds and still stranger occupants of those worlds, plus a real Devil, one who—until he ran into the full fury of a woman—seemed to have at least nine lives.

When the bottle arrived, Longarm poured for both of them and lifted his glass. "Chief," he said, "I propose a toast."

Vail lifted his glass.

"To the Celestials. May they soon be sailing past the Dragon's Eye and through fleets of junks on the Pearl River delta. May they see again the rice fields and the Pagoda of Nine Stories."

"What in the hell are you talkin' about?"

"Will you drink to it?"

Vail shrugged. "Sure. Why not?"

Both men threw the rye down their gullet and Longarm leaned back to light his cheroot, a distant look in his eyes. He was wondering if Miguel Sanchez would be able to find a place for himself in that distant land.

He sure as hell hoped so.